The author is a retired University Senior Lecturer, teaching a BA (Hons) course in Graphic Design. He lives with his wife on Merseyside, where he was born.

Apart from his writing, he is a musician and composer and long-time boater and caravanner.

To my son, Michael and his wife, Helen.

R.E. Bowden

NO QUARTER GIVEN

AUSTIN MACAULEY PUBLISHERS™

LONDON • CAMBRIDGE • NEW YORK • SHARJAH

A CIP catalogue record for this title is available from the British Library.

ISBN 9781035841493 (Paperback)
ISBN 9781035841509 (ePub e-book)

www.austinmacauley.com

First Published 2024
Austin Macauley Publishers Ltd®
1 Canada Square
Canary Wharf
London
E14 5AA

Thanks to the editorial staff for knocking my poor story into something worth publishing!

Tables of Contents

Chapter One

I arrived in Liverpool early in the morning. It was raining hard and the normally fabulous riverside view, from the upper deck of the Irish Ferry, was obscured. There was a raw and freezing cold wind, too. I shivered and went back down to the bar. For some reason, I knew I had a tough day ahead of me. I was not wrong.

The bar wasn't open, of course. It was just after seven am. So I sat on one of the stools and gazed into space. I did this a lot.

I should explain. I'd been in Ireland for a year, recuperating after being invalided out of the Royal Navy. As the eldest son of an Earl, The Honourable Benjamin Hawke, no less, I was not short of money. My family was stupidly rich, God knows. I had a bank card with unlimited funds behind it.

Lucky old me, of course, but it meant I had no ambition and it pandered to my inherent laziness. Why should I work?

I had had a good time in Ireland. It's a great country to spend time in, just lazing about and doing nothing except enjoying myself as best as I could. This was largely chatting up the girls, boozing, gambling, fighting, that sort of thing. Trying to forget. I told no-one of my title, of course, just answered to "Ben".

I'd spent all my adult life in the Royal Navy, and being *The Hon*. Benjamin Hawke, as said, probably helped me to rise quickly through the ranks to be a senior officer, a Commander actually, and proud of it. I loved every minute of it. And I saw a lot of action.

As a big guy, well over six feet tall and athletic, I was seconded to the SBS, Special Boat Service—the equivalent of the Army SAS, and I did many covert missions, landing by night from a sub into enemy territory. Really exciting stuff. I enjoyed it.

Then it happened, a disaster. On one of those missions, in the Middle East, I had suffered a bad head injury—shrapnel from a roadside bomb—and consequentially had to spend months in hospital, undergoing reconstructive surgery. I recovered to a great extent, thankfully, but then had to spend a period of convalescence, in a superb private clinic in Switzerland. Followed by the year in Ireland.

I was now fully fit *physically*, but mentally—well, brain damage is never fully recoverable, so my career was over, permanently, which I hated and found it all very difficult, coping with my new, enforced idle life, such as it was. I was grieving for my previous life, of course. I always will.

Now here I was, back in England, footloose and fancy free, as they say. In fact, I was feeling useless. A big, useless lump, no good for anything. A fighter, a trained unarmed-combat killer, not needed in civvy street. I was a bit worried that if I was involved in a serious fight, my training would kick in and my ruthless killer mode would take over.

The mantra for the SBS was: *no quarter given and none asked* (However, the Irish, bless them, liked to finish a boozy night with an enjoyable barney, but that was more a friendly

sort of thing, very few wild swings actually landed!).
Anyway, as said, I sat on that stool and numbly gazed into
space.

Then my mobile rang, which was very surprising, as 99%
of the time it was switched off. I had charged it up last night,
in case I needed a taxi, and I must have drunkenly left it on.
Anyway, it rang, so, like you do, I pressed the key and said,
'Hello?'

The answer came, 'Is that you, Ben?'

It was my brother, Charles. I hadn't been in touch with my
brother or my father all the while I had been in Ireland. I had
just wanted peace and quiet. They had no idea where I was,
as I had not told them. The last they heard from me was when
I was in Switzerland, a year ago.

Not that I did not love them both to bits, I did. I suppose
it was just me trying to forget the horrors and not wanting to
talk about it. A brain injury is a funny thing. PTSD—
nightmares, hallucinations—nasty. I didn't want to think
about it. Ever.

Anyway, as I said, it was Charles, so I mumbled
something about meaning to get in touch, but hadn't got
around to it yet, when he cut me off, sharply.

'OK, Ben, OK, fine, relax, that's fine. Look, where are
you?'

I told him. He said he would be with me as soon as he
could. 'Stay there,' he said. 'I have something to tell you. It's
very important.' He rang off.

Charles and I have always been very close over the years,
until the last year, of course. He is also big and athletic. We
had a lot in common growing up in our stately home in
Lancashire, now given into the care of the National Trust,

thank God. Since his marriage to Nancy and them having two kids, we had drifted apart a bit, but had been still pretty close buddies.

He had stayed with Father helping him to run the vast estates we had, and the various businesses, whereas I just wanted to join the navy and see the world. He was thirty-two, I was thirty-four.

I reckoned it would take a good hour or more for Charles to find me, I told him I would be in the café on the terminal building on the Landing Stage where the Mersey Ferry docked. The Irish Ferry docked somewhere different I knew. I didn't really know Liverpool that well, although I had been there every year when I could for the racing at Aintree, the wonderful Grand National, which is why I was there.

Incidentally, my father owns a string of racehorses, and one of his horses was the bookies' favourite (Nugget) for the race, so I'll be supporting that, of course. Charles will be there as well as Father, so we will have a good day.

The family had traditionally booked some suites at the old Adelphi Hotel again, now much reduced in status, but still good. *Charles, with his "important" news, might alter my plan, such as it was*, I thought. Actually, I enjoyed going to the races, but only as a punter, not an owner; didn't want the fuss and bother of all that. Just have a flutter and a few drinks with the family, perhaps chat up a few ladies, that's always been me.

Time dragged on. An hour passed. I bought a sandwich and coffee. Not bad. Some instinct made me go out and look outside, and lucky I did, as I recognised the tall figure of Brother Charles walking towards me. I raised my arm in greeting. He did the same. I beckoned him over and after

14

shaking hands warmly, he followed me back to my table in the café.

I thought he looked very young and handsome. He was wearing a grey suit and tie, like he always prefers to do.

I ordered two more coffees. *Charles, close up, looked tired and strained*, I thought, *but he was obviously pleased to see me, as I was to see him, of course.*

I said, 'So what's this important thing you've rushed here to tell me, Charles? Wife and kids OK?'

'They're fine, Ben. No, it's nothing to do with them. I'm really sorry to have to tell you like this, but it's Father, I'm afraid. Look, I've moved heaven and earth trying to contact you, even hired detectives, but...'

I butted in, 'What about him?' I said, as a ball of ice found its way into my stomach. It was obvious what was coming.

'He's dead, Ben.'

'What? What? Dead? Oh my God, no! He can't be, he's fitter than you or me. He's...'

'It was a hunting accident, his horse fell and rolled on him. He broke his neck. If he had lived, he would have been a quadriplegic. But he didn't make the hospital, died on the spot.'

I stuttered, 'Christ NO! NO!...Father **DEAD**?...I can't BELIEVE it, Charles. I've...I've b...been in Dublin all the time since leaving Switzerland. You...d...don't get much English news. I didn't read the papers...I...I had no idea.' My voice tailed off. I felt sick, rushed to the café toilet and half-collapsed, wedged in one of the tiny cubicles.

After a few minutes, I felt calm enough to stand up and I staggered over to a basin and tried to splash cold water on my face. The damn tap kept putting itself off, one of those spring-loaded types. I swore luridly, under my breath. Anyway, after several attempts I felt a bit better, dried my face on a paper towel and went back in the café.

Charles had, sensibly, left me to get over it, rather than following me. He still sat at the table, staring into space. I felt sorry for him.

As I joined him, something hit me hard in the guts. I realised that I was now The Fucking Seventeenth Earl of Sumerton, succeeding my father to the ancient title. It was the last thing I wanted. My father was—had been—still quite a young man, not yet sixty. I had reasoned that he would live to his nineties, and would never retire, so no problem.

I thought it would be many, many years before I had the awesome responsibility of being in charge of the estate, the villages, the companies, here and abroad, the hundreds of staff. I very nearly rushed back to the toilets but managed to fight the feeling off as I sat down heavily, opposite my brother. I felt my life had finished. I didn't think I could cope with it all.

I really felt suicidal at that moment, but I forced a ghost of a grin, and croaked, 'So what now, Charles. What now?'

'If you are up to it, I'm going to drive you back to my home, Charles. There's a lot to discuss now you have inherited the title, as you must realise. My car is parked not too far away, so fetch your luggage and we'll be off.'

So that's what we did. I only had one small case and a backpack, in all a few pairs of jeans and tee-shirts, a few sweaters, shorts, socks, etc., nothing much at all. I had hoped to stay like that forever. No chance now. None at all. I thought it couldn't get worse. It did.

Chapter Two

The journey to my brother's home was uneventful, although the traffic was a pain, as usual. Charles was a slow and careful driver. The car, a Range Rover, was warm and comfortable and the conversation was sparse. Charles was not a chatty type of guy, like me, both of us are quite happy not talking at all for long periods of time.

I felt myself nodding off several times. Father's demise was not mentioned at all. I wasn't ready to talk about it, as my brother obviously realised.

On the journey, I thought about my title. The original Earl was a notorious privateer—a sort of legalised Pirate of the seven seas. He captured a lot of Spanish merchant ships, loaded with Mexican gold, making a fortune for Queen Elizabeth I. She made him an Earl and gave him a lot of Lancashire in return.

An early portrait of him looked very like me today. Big, swashbuckling and swarthy-looking, with an aggressive stance. He was a ruthless tyrant of the seas. He stole the gold, sold the captured ships—and the Spanish sailors, those he hadn't killed in battle, of course. I quite admired him, to be honest. Proud even. Envious? Maybe.

I should mention, Mother died many years ago, when Charles and I were quite small. Breast cancer. I cannot really remember her. Father never re-married and never mentioned her name. Photographs and paintings show that she was remarkably beautiful, though.

Sad, I suppose, but children of our class were sent away to boarding school at an early age, didn't see much of their parents, and nanny was really a sort of surrogate mother and father for us.

We eventually pulled up in the driveway outside the house, which was a modern, large and quite attractive-looking place built in the grounds of the family estate in the late 1990s. Nancy and Charles elected not to stay in the big house, which, as said, now belonged to the National Trust. I don't blame them.

Father had more or less stopped living there too, and in the few times he was at home, he had stayed with Charles and Nancy. Their charming house with its large garden, was in a remote part of the grounds, not open to the public of course.

Charles strode ahead of me and opened the front door. The house was empty because Nancy was at work; she was a doctor at the local hospital, the kids were at school. There were no staff living in, apart from lovely old nanny. Charles liked cooking and regarded himself as quite a good chef. I wasn't so sure, but it beat Navy fare, I suppose.

Nothing was going to happen that day, so after a sandwich lunch, we just did our own thing for the afternoon. I went for a walk in the grounds, with the dogs. The dogs, four of them, all Jack Russell, were for their noisy security, but they were good friends too, and loved. The kids were brought home by nanny at around four o'clock.

They rather ignored me, largely because they really did not know me very well and it had been at least eighteen months ago the last time I was there—a long time in a small child's life. It was nice hearing them laughing and playing about though. I probably frightened them a bit, looking as I did.

Nancy arrived about an hour later. I like Nancy a lot, always have. She is strong, bright, clever, attractive and friendly. Everyone liked her. She gave me a hug and then rushed off to find her brood. I heard them laughing and playing all together, with Charles there too, and the dogs.

I felt rather envious, I must admit, though the idea of settling down was far from my mind. I'd never met anyone that I wanted to spend the rest of my life with, but I lived in a faint hope that the right woman would come along one day. I doubt if any woman would have me anyway. I would not be easy to live with after fifteen years in the Royal Navy, where I expected my ratings to do what I wanted, when I wanted it, how I wanted it and jump to it.

Ireland had been good for me in that respect. The Irish can't be bossed about. No way. They don't take life that seriously on the whole, with a few exceptions. They have this expression: 'Ah, it's all a load of flubber!' I admire and envy them.

The next few days were spent in meetings with lawyers, managers, various officials all telling me about what it meant for me to be in charge now that my father had passed away. I found it, frankly, a horrible experience. I really hated every minute of it. I was to be Chair of the Main Committee where I would have to make lots of decisions and sign lots of documents.

These decisions were vital to the running of the estate, etc., I was told, and would "trickle down" to various other committees or whatever. It was very baffling to a simple sailor like me. I mean I have had a good education, typical of my class, and have a first-class honours degree in Military History from Oxford, but all that has not fitted me for a top management role at all.

Really, I am an action man sort of guy, rather than someone stuck behind a big desk. I'm just not suited for this life at all. But I smiled and nodded my head and did my best not to look too stupid. I know a lot of those guys were worried about me, and didn't blame them.

On my credit side, I was used to being in charge and making decisions. Very different kind of decisions, but *decisions* nevertheless. It began to get easier as I started to understand the job a bit better. Father actually was not that involved in day-to-day estate running of course.

Just the big decisions, so not so bad so long as I understood what was at stake and I reckon with a lot of help— I'm a fast learner—I'd cope. Also, I rather hoped to lean a lot on Brother Charles and persuade him to deputise for me; often.

***

Then, disaster struck. Not at work, at my brother's home.

It was a Friday. The kids did not turn up when nanny went to collect them from school. After frantic searches revealed nothing, a message was sent to Nancy at the hospital. Of course, she rushed back to take charge of the situation. She rang the police and a constable was sent, followed by an inspector, as the family has a lot of influence. A search party was set up to search the school and the grounds. Nothing.

Charles and Nancy were going frantic. The police inspector, a quiet, efficient sort of guy, grey haired, stocky, round face, did his best to calm the situation. He told us his name was Inspector Wallis.

He said, 'If it is of any comfort, we do have a lot of kids disappearing and in nine out of ten cases, they are discovered somewhere and returned within the first day. Kids can sometimes just go and hide for fun, or because they are angry with their parents, or they can just run away for a bit of excitement. Often the reasons they give don't make much sense to adults. Let's face it, they're kids!'

Nancy said, 'I think they have been kidnapped.' She was just about holding herself together, but the strain on her face told a story.

The inspector said that this was very unlikely. Such things did not happen in this country, he suggested. *This was probably correct*, I thought.

The inspector eventually left us in peace, promising that everything will be alright, wait and see. But he was wrong.

The phone rang. Nancy rushed to answer it and as she listened, she went white with shock. The phone fell from her fingers. I managed to pick it up, nearly bumping into Charles who went straight over to comfort his wife. She struggled to speak but gasped, 'They've got the boys.'

I held the phone to my ear. It was a recorded message, in an electronic voice:

We have your boys. They are unharmed and quite safe. Do not worry. I will give you the details of a bank account. If you simply transfer the sum of five million pounds into that account, your boys will be returned to you fit and well, at once.

There followed the bank account details, with the currency to be in bitcoin. The message ended and then repeated, endlessly apparently.

Charles and Nancy looked at me. I passed the phone to Charles. He listened intently.

Nancy said, desperately, 'Just pay it, Charles. Pay it now.'

Five million pounds probably sounds a lot to you, but to Charles and Nancy, it was a drop in the ocean. Among the companies we own are several merchant banks, so hey!

Charles just nodded and went out to his office to make the payment. It was as simple as that.

We heard nothing else that day, but the following morning, we had another message. It told us that the boys were at a service station café on the M6 and had been told to sit at a table and had been provided with coke and burgers, and to wait to be picked up by their parents.

Of course, we rushed off at once and fair enough, there they were, happy as larks with several cans of coke and what looked like the remains of several burgers. It was a MacDonalds outlet. They couldn't wait to tell us of their big adventure and were looking forward to tell the same tale to their friends at school, too.

The kidnappers had treated them very well, given them fifty pounds, and had played football with them, and they had slept in a motor caravan, and had played board games, and had stayed up late. The words tumbled and stumbled out. Their rosy faces showed how much they had enjoyed being kidnapped!

Charles and Nancy refused to tell the police anything at all and told the kids not to tell anyone about being kidnapped. It took a long while to convince them and they were really disappointed, but they were good kids, and intelligent, so they realised eventually that it was what they had to do. I did not interfere, but it was at that point that I realised that I had a job to do.

I wanted to find those bastard kidnappers, punish them, and bring them to justice, or kill them, no quarter. It had got personal. They had harmed my family. I also told Charles about my intentions but he did not comment. Looking back, I wish I hadn't told Charles.

What I did not realise at the time was that the kidnappers had bugged his house. I was to find this out the hard way.

Chapter Three

Charles rang the police and said the boys had been found safe and well. He made up some story which satisfied them apparently.

In my chosen new role, I went back to the motorway service station and tried to interview the staff, but they did not want to know. They were just too busy to be bothered. It was at that point that I realised how difficult it was going to be. Unless I was a policeman, no-one would want to be interviewed. I had to think again.

Then I had an idea—perhaps I could open up a business as a private detective! It solved a big problem for me in that it would give me, I thought, *a purpose in life, after no longer being in the Forces. I rather fancied myself as a PI!*

When I told my brother, he had a good laugh. I don't think he took me seriously at all, nor did his wife who also thought the idea of an Earl becoming a private investigator was hilarious. I rather agreed with that, but I thought I would have to use another name and hide my title. It was all very early days. Again, I later regretted saying anything about my plans in that house.

I continued to be a guest at the house and continued getting to grips with my new way of life as head of a vast group of companies. *Charles and Nancy also got on with their lives but brought in a security firm to keep a close eye on the kids, which was sensible of them*, I thought.

I found out much later that many super rich families, especially abroad, have to spend vast sums to prevent such crimes as kidnapping of themselves or their family. This information came when I became involved in my quest to bring the kidnappers of my family to book, but, as said, this was a lot later.

Now, while I was thinking about becoming a PI, as I say, life carried on and I also had to think about the forthcoming races at Aintree, as this was the reason I had come to England in the first place, as said! What I now realised was that, as I now was the owner of Nugget, the bookmaker's favourite horse to win the celebrated Grand National race, I would have to be more high-profile.

As such I would need to attend, of course, and I would have to be involved in a lot of protocol as the owner, media interviews, etc. This was pretty depressing. Not my thing at all. But I had to do my duty.

So a few days later, I booked some time off and went to stay at the lovely old Adelphi Hotel in Liverpool. I always had the same suite of rooms, delightfully old fashioned but quite luxurious in a faded way. The bathroom was superb, exactly as it was when the place was built in the early years of the last century.

A huge white-enamelled cast-iron bath and monstrous brass taps. I loved it. Sheer bliss to soak in, reading a racing magazine. Much more pleasant than a shower, surely.

To be fair, the hotel had seen better days, but it still retained its old-world charm, having never been modernised. At the time of the Aintree meeting, it was full to the rafters with racegoers of all nations, but largely the Irish and the Arabs joining the English in a wonderful mix. I loved the atmosphere of the place and the long history.

The staff were great too, full of "scouse humour". To those who don't know, Liverpudlians are sometimes called "scousers" named after a type of lamb stew, "scouse", which was, historically, a famous local cheap but nutritious meal. Scousers are known for their quick wit and basic humour and for their friendliness and hearts of gold. In my view: "the salt of the earth".

Charles and Nancy had always attended the race with my father, but not this time. The kidnapping had shaken them to the core. Of course, I understood, but I now had to face everyone and the media all by myself. I told myself I just had to do it and get on with it.

So the great day arrived. I dressed in a lounge suit, as the race was not a big social affair like Ascot, for instance, no top hats needed. I thought, *how bad can it be?* Little did I know, it was a day that would change my life.

I did my duty at the course (*noblesse oblige* and all that). I tried my best to be friendly and pleasant, I smiled, touched elbows (Covid), thanked folk for their sympathy about the loss of my father. They told me how much they all missed him. I just wished to hell he hadn't died and that he and Charles would be there to do the honours.

But, I got on with it as best I could, as said. There was no option.

I went and talked to my trainer and jockey and wished them both well. I have never been involved with the stables in the past, being a full-time sailor, and I hoped that Charles would soon be able to carry on in that capacity. *If not, maybe*

I would sell the stables, I thought. I patted my horse, the favourite, the massive stallion we called "Nugget". I am not particularly a horse person myself, despite my background, but I must admit the beautiful creature's velvety nose was nice to pat.

I made some jolly comments, probably foolish, but people were kind to me. I know jockeys and trainers hate owners that interfere with them and offer probably stupid suggestions, so I kept it short.

I escaped back to the main concourse. The champagne was flowing, the noise deafening, the fine rain relentless. My tolerance level was getting dangerously low. My brain injury did not take stress well at all, I knew. I started to blame the bastard kidnappers. *That was why Charles was not there.* He was looking after his family.

I even blamed the kidnappers for being the reason my father was not there, which in a more rational frame of mind I would have realised was nonsense, of course, but I felt anger boiling up inside me. There is a lot of anger in me, buried deep. I loved the Navy, loved my career, I was still grieving for my loss. I urgently needed a refuge for some peace and quiet.

I headed for the VIP lounge and found a quiet(ish) corner, away from blaring TV screens and PA screams. I picked up a racing paper and hid behind it, pretending to read, like a detective in an old film. It was baking hot in there, but thankfully smoke free, unlike the days before the cigars and fags were banned, when it would have been hard to see through the fog. Never smoked in my life. Never appealed, somehow.

I'm used to some discomfort, being a sailor. No problem there, but I wished I could escape and get out. Right out of Aintree, but with my horse being the favourite, I had no realistic chance. If Nugget won, I would really be in big trouble. I reckon my face told a story of deep gloom, half-hidden as it was.

A female voice said, 'Ben Hawke! How lovely! I've just heard you are a Duke or something. What are you doing skulking behind a newspaper in a corner?'

The low, husky Irish voice was unmistakeable. I put aside the paper and looked up. God, she was gorgeous! Some Irish girls are amazing, black hair, perfect complexion, stunning figure and huge, golden-flecked eyes, "put in with a smutty finger", as they say over there. Of course, I remembered her well.

I had been one of her conquests in Dublin about a month ago. Note "one of *her* conquests". She had obviously fancied me for some reason and had pursued me relentlessly at the racecourse over there. What red-blooded male can resist for long a determined and beautiful woman? It was the typical booze-soaked one-night-stand, yes, but a night I will always remember, that!

I didn't think I would ever see her again and that was fine for both of us. And now here she was, looking absolutely incredible, dressed to kill for the big occasion in a figure-hugging red creation.

I wondered what billionaire's arm she would be clutching this time, as I mumbled a reply to her, indicating she should sit down opposite me. She was carrying two glasses of bubbly in her pretty little white hands. Now I have nothing against predatory women flaunting their charms to get what they want

28

in any way shape or form. It makes the world a happier place, surely.

Anyway, there she was, sitting down opposite me, squirming to get comfortable, showing off her alluring curves. Not a thin girl, not like a model, all skinny and skeletal. Who wants to cuddle a skeleton? Not me.

I realised I could not remember her name, if indeed I ever knew it. It was like that in Ireland, everything laid back and casual, as said.

So I said, 'Hey!' (I'm not the most brilliant conversationalist).

She said, 'Hey yourself!' (Not exactly Jane Austen dialogue, this).

She added, 'The name you're *not* trying very hard to remember is Sue, OK?'

I grinned. I relaxed a bit. She chuckled, low and sexy.

'Hey, Sue.'

'Hey, Duke Ben.'

'I'm not a Duke, silly.'

She sipped her drink, gorgeous eyes unblinking.

'Come on, I know you're like, aristocratic, or whatever.'

I confessed to being an Earl. I rose to my size 13 feet, towering above her. I don't know why I did this. Perhaps, anyway, it was a bit late. I should have risen to my feet immediately she had spoken to me I suppose, being a gentleman.

'I do remember how big you were, Ben,' she murmured. 'You've no need to demonstrate.' Her expression was bland, but I knew what she really meant. I sat down again. I think the word is: *nonplussed.* I was way out of my league and floundering.

She took pity on me.

'Look, Ben,' she said, 'talk to me. You're the best thing I've come across all day so far. I've been bored to tears, much as I adore horses, and racing. I am IRISH, after all. Oh my, you look so gorgeous in a suit and tie. I'm beginning to feel really randy, my Lord.'

There was that chuckle again. I got the feeling that she was not impressed by my title at all. She was having fun, playing with me.

I said, 'I'm sorry, Sue. It's really great to see you. It's just that everything has gone pear-shaped for me recently.'

'Tell me all about it.'

Rather to my own amazement, I did. I told her about my father's death, my brother's kids' kidnapped, my bomb injury and the loss of my naval career, the lot. She just listened quietly. She reached across and touched my clenched fist.

I really was astonished at myself, opening my heart to someone who I had considered, really, as just an inconsequential one-day fling sort of person. But the way she looked at me, with those "tender eyes a'shine". I felt a warmth grow inside me, giving me a sort of comfort. Crazy.

She said, 'Thanks for telling me all that, Ben. It's probably helped getting it all off your chest like that. It must have been horrible for you.' She paused and looked out towards the windows. 'Look, the rain has stopped and the sun is shining. Let's have a walk outside, the big race will be starting soon.'

'But,' I stammered, 'who are you with? Surely you are not on your own?'

'I'm with you, Ben, and I have a feeling it will be for a long time.' She gave me a lovely secret smile.

She rose to her feet on her very high heels. A vision. She had said *I'm with you*—I couldn't believe how much that had delighted me. Me, a big tough sailor. I got up and followed her softly-swaying body out through the door into the sunshine. Outside, she put her arm through mine, bodies touching, those thrilling curves nudging against me.

Something happened to me at that moment, something so unexpected, it knocked me sideways:

Joy.

Chapter Four

We strolled around together, greeting people, some of whom looked at me curiously as they had never seen me with a woman companion before, I suppose. Over the years, I had met many regulars who knew my father and had seen me and my brother growing up. Most of them knew my name and also knew I had succeeded my father to the title.

Some officials even touched their caps to me. Some said, 'My Lord,' rather to my discomfort, even though I had now got used to it back at the estate, of course. Sue had just smiled and nodded.

I wondered how she felt. I was feeling weird, probably due to emotion at telling my tale of woe to this beautiful woman by my side, plus the champagne and lack of food. I had never in my life had a girlfriend as such. Never saw the need. Or the interest.

I was rather tied up just with myself to be honest. But today, everything had changed I realised. I really wanted this woman for myself, for keeps. I needed her! Badly!

Suddenly, as our bodies kept bumping against each other, my hard and angular one and her soft and pliant one, I started to grow hard "down below" and it was urgent and uncontrollable. I made an excuse to leave her, saying I would be back in a few minutes, to stay where she was, please. This had never happened to me before, even when I was very young.

I headed for the VIP lounge, limping a bit. I would run cold water over my wrists—an old trick—and then sit in a loo closet for a while to cool my ardour, so to speak, not that I had any idea whether it would work, but I had to do something, and quick. From the expression on her face, I think she knew exactly what was wrong, for she gave me a mischievous grin and that lovely chuckle.

It didn't help one bit! Oh, and as for the exotic perfume in her glossy hair…Oh God! I was in big trouble. Could be messy.

Off I limped as fast as I could manage. Back in the lounge, the cold water did certainly help to quiet things down. I headed for a closet. The lounge was more or less empty I noticed, as the big race was just about to start. I did see a couple of heavy-set characters standing around, out of the corner of my eye. They did not look like the usual VIP types, I registered, somewhere in the back of my brain.

As I came to the door of the first, generously spacious VIP cubicle, I was shoved hard in my back and grabbed violently by both my arms, forcing my head down the toilet bowl. I felt a sharp pain in my back, like a knife was being used.

Then my years of unarmed-combat training came to my aid. I kicked back with all my strength, low, wide, and hard. I heard some choice swear words. Really those two stupid thugs were no match for me. I simply twisted around and thrust upwards with both knees and feet. They went flying, grunting with pain.

I was enjoying myself. The obscenities were quite interesting. I could have killed both thugs with ease, but

33

thankfully, I managed to resist the impulse. One really just can't go and kill people in the VIP lounge at Aintree Racecourse! Not done.

I thought fast. Surely this was not a simple mugging? Was this something to do with the kidnappers? Had I been targeted for a kicking to warn me off, perhaps? I got to my feet, ready to question these thugs, probably just hired muscle doing what they had been told to do. This could be a break-through.

Unfortunately, at this point, two burly guards rushed in. The two scallies lashed at them and limped quickly to the outer door, but were grabbed by more security staff running in. Now there were six of them crowded in, come to join in the fun, no doubt.

Muggings are common enough almost anywhere and this is what they immediately assumed was happening. I wondered how these two had got in in the first place—and into the VIP lounge no less.

One of the security staff recognised me. I knew his name, Ted. After all, I had been coming to this meeting since I was a small boy and Ted is no chicken. He was a real Liverpool scouser, curly black hair, *Viva Zapata* moustache, heavily built with a beer belly and an inexhaustible supply of jokes, mostly of the sort you couldn't tell your sister, so to speak.

Ted said, in his "extremely-rare" accent, 'Hi, Benny, oh…er…sorry, hello, my Lord. Like, what's goin' on? Er, like?'

I said, 'Hello, Ted, nice to see you. I think these two scallies have just tried to mug me. I want a word with them, in private, don't call in the police just yet please.'

'OK, fair enough, your lordship. We know those two characters well enough and we couldn't understand how they had passes, like, but passes they had, like, so we had to let them in. We've got them cuffed together so they are pretty safe, though it looks to me, like, you were doing alright by yourself, Sir!' Ted grinned at me. I grinned back.

There was a roar outside. The race had started but I tried to ignore it. I needed a quick word with the two thugs first. I squatted down in front of one of them who looked a bit more intelligent. His mouth was open in his pig-like face showing uneven brown teeth, some missing. I put my fist in front of his face and threatened him with more violence.

I said, 'Look, I want answers. You have been paid to rough me up and give me a message, right?' He was obviously in a lot of pain.

He snarled, thickly, 'Youse gorra lay off, or else, like. This Chinky scon paid us to do you over a bit and warn you to mind your own fucking business or the next time they'll fucking kill you and your fucking family, like.'

'I thought as much,' I said, smiling.

After more threats from me, they told me they did not know who the "Chinky" was (their word) but the money was good. They had been given five hundred pounds and passes to the racetrack, with another five hundred pounds to come.

I knew I would get nothing more from them, so I left them to the security staff to deal with. They asked me to contact them at their office as soon as the race finished, or as soon as I could get away and that the police would take over and would need a statement from me sometime.

Ted met me outside. He said, 'Your horse came in third, my Lord, so congratulations! But, look here, Sir, you look awful, blood down your neck, ear bloody and blood on your shirt front. You can't go to the awards ceremony looking like that. I think you need a doctor, Sir, if I may say so. Is that a knife wound on your back?'

'Just a little nick, I think, Ted. I'll go and tidy myself up a bit inside the VIP lounge, there's soap and towels, etc. No, I'm fine, don't you worry, but thanks! I'll have to dash.'

I looked in a mirror. A sorry sight to behold, suit torn, shirt and tie in a mess. I took off my jacket and shirt and washed myself as quick as I could. Those thugs had flushed the loo on my head, which didn't help. I put my clothes back on and combed my hair. I inspected the result. Horrible!

But I had to turn up to that ceremony. I could hear the PA lady calling for me urgently. I dashed over there. A young female constable ran alongside me asking me to come and give a statement afterwards at the police hut. I agreed and she went off.

The thing that really was upsetting me now, was that I imagined that the lovely Sue would be thinking I had dumped her. She had probably gone home in a huff. I had no idea of her surname or anything about her apart from the fact she was Irish. As I ran, I looked all around, hoping to catch sight of her. Nothing.

I clambered stiffly on to the awards ceremony stage, apologising profusely as I did. I got some very funny looks, no doubt at my appearance. But British good manners prevailed, and nobody commented. To be fair, the Irish, Arabs and other nationals were equally good-mannered. How civilised…

Actually, I was not the centre of attraction anyway, for the media or anyone else. The winning horse belonged to Tony McGuire, no less, the billionaire "rock god". This incredibly handsome guy was the one everybody wanted. I was a nobody. Earls are ten a penny at Aintree Racecourse. And that was great.

I accepted my trophy cup and cheque, and as soon as I could, sidled away. I was not feeling too good, to be fair, a knock on the head could be disastrous, the doctors had told me so. I was shattered and just wanted to go back to the Adelphi, soak in a bath and sleep. I managed to offload the cup to one of the stable lads.

But next, I needed to go and give a statement, so I dutifully went to the mobile police unit and after a lot of fuss and bother, did the necessary. They wanted to charge the two thugs with common assault and battery but I refused to co-operate as I just wanted the thing over. I would not press charges, so the police really had to let them go.

They were not happy, the police. I did not see the two scallies again, nor did I want to.

I was not happy that the Chinese community seemed to be involved. You really do not want to mess with the Chinese. Those Tongs make the Italian Mafia mob seem like babies-in-arms. Something to think about. There is a big Chinese community in Liverpool, I knew. The police never interfere. There is never any trouble. Now there might be.

Chapter Five

I was in a foul mood. Now the kidnappers had made me lose the girl of my dreams as well as giving my family a terrible shock and making us pay a lot of money, not to mention my aching head and painful back. I was furious.

Really the worst thing was losing contact with Sue. I had never felt like this about a woman before, and it was eating away in my gut. I could not imagine any way of finding her again. Some detective me!

An hour's soak in the bath helped a bit. I fell asleep in the water though and when I woke up, it was cold. I got out, wrapped myself in a huge towel and went through to the bedroom. I half-collapsed on the bed and went to sleep again.

When I woke up, hours later, it was dark outside. I felt a lot better. My headache had more or less subsided and my other cuts and scratches had stopped bleeding. They really were nothing.

I made myself a cup of coffee, ate a biscuit, thought about dinner. Then the doorbell went.

To my astonishment, it was Sue! And she was smiling!

'So what happened to you, Ben? You look awful!' She said, pushing past me and into the room. She sat on one of the massive armchairs.

I stammered, 'Sue! This is great. How did you find me? Look, I was attacked by a couple of thugs, hired by those bastard kidnappers. I spent ages looking for you afterwards but I gave up eventually. And here you are. I can't tell you how sorry I am for all this. Where are you staying, then?'

'Next door, Ben, would you believe!'

'What here, at the Adelphi? I don't believe it.'

'Yes, I'm staying in the next suite to you. You have not the faintest idea who I am, have you?'

I sat on the bed and looked at her. 'No, not the faintest. Tell me.'

'Well, my name is Sue McGuire, does that help?'

I gazed at her in astonishment. 'McGuire? Oh my God, do you mean like *Tony McGuire*, the famous musician; are you his daughter, or what?'

'Got it in one, Ben! I'm one of five! Daddy is staying here too but we are going home first thing tomorrow. John Lennon airport, in Daddy's lovely little private jet. Daddy is a qualified pilot y'know.' She grinned at me.

'But, but…' I started.

'Don't worry, you won't get rid of me that easily, Ben. We have a big estate near Dublin. I want you to come and join me there. Soon. We don't get too many English Naval hero Earls, you know. My sisters and mummy are dying to meet you, as is Daddy.' She gave one of her chuckles, deep down low and sexy.

She added, 'And *you* are taking me out to dinner tonight, too, whether you want to or not! It's booked for seven-thirty, so get your glad rags on.' She rose up in one graceful motion and moved to the door. She waved, 'See you here, then.' She was gone. I just sat and stared. I had a feeling I'd been hooked, rod, line and sinker. And it was marvellous.

So that night, we went out on the town. Not something I've really ever done before. And that night, what was left of it, we shared a bed, next door. Incredible night. I really could not believe what was happening to me. Fantastic sex. She really knew how to please me. Drove me crazy. It was like a fabulous dream.

I did not want to wake up.

Chapter Six

The next day, Sue had gone early. I did not see her, but I had her details, telephone number, address in Ireland, email address, the lot. And she had mine. We arranged that I would come and stay for a weekend, in a few weeks' time, *as a first step* as she said. *A first step to what*, I wondered, *worriedly*.

I still felt I was in a dream, but I went back to my brother's house that day, and over the next couple of days got down to the business of being the Seventeenth Earl of Sumerton.

Things on the estate were by now fairly-well settled. So, I decided, with Charles' help, to take a few days off to concentrate on my plans to become a private detective. I had spent time on the Internet and read a couple of books, but I really had made little progress.

I thought that what I needed was some help and I kept thinking about an old pal of mine from the Navy, Lieutenant Ian Jones, my "oppo" as we sailors called them, from "opposite number": a mate, a close friend, someone to rely on, at your side in battle. His parents owned a hotel in Llandudno, a seaside resort in North Wales. I knew his parents quite well, as I had stayed with them several times over the years.

They were grand people. Incidentally, they normally all spoke Welsh at home, naturally enough in North Wales.

I thought, *why not visit his parents? A surprise.* They would know how to contact him, because, I reckoned, he could be anywhere in the world, being a Navy man. He and I had shared many of the actions where the SBS had been involved. I had once saved his life. He saved mine at the time I got the injury that invalided me out.

But we had inevitably lost touch while I was recovering in Ireland and Switzerland. I hadn't seen him since the first days after my wounding when he had stayed at my side for days, as I lay hovering between life and death. I love that man. No other word.

You never know, I thought, *I could be lucky.* He might be based here in the UK at someplace or other? Shore-based. Sailors are not always at sea. Anyway, I wanted a few days in Wales, too. My favourite country in the world.

So, I borrowed one of the estate staff cars, a Range Rover, and set off the next day. Not really a long journey and a familiar route. I stopped for lunch on the way in a country pub and it was really good. I was relaxed and happy as a lark.

By three o'clock, I was travelling along the A55, admiring the view of the lovely countryside and the gorgeous Welsh hills. Before long, I reached the fine old seaside resort of Llandudno and steered the car slowly along the promenade.

The sun was shining on the calm blue water of the bay, trillions of tiny points of light shimmering on the water. Superb. I just love the sea. I found a good carpark, and decided to walk to Ian's family hotel, which was on the front, not far from the pier. The air felt fresh and salty, with no wind to speak of. I strode out purposely.

I was dressed in jeans and a navy-blue tee shirt. I noticed some very young girls giggling away on a prom bench. I looked across and they waved at me, and I waved back, to more giggles. I was pleased, to be truthful. I was proud of my big, muscular body. Why not? Enjoy it while you can, is my motto. Life is short.

Now I had a smile on my face. Isn't life grand! Enjoy the moment. *Seize the day*—all that type of thing. I was due for a fall, of course. Never tempt fate, is another good motto. Pride goes before a fall, they say. Somebody up there looks down and goes 'Zap! That'll teach him.'

What soon wiped that smile from my face was just a few minutes' walk away along the prom. The hotel owned by my mate Ian's family hove into view, and to my horror, I saw a large sign saying "FOR SALE—hotel business and premises." I ran up the steps and entered, going straight to the reception desk.

There was nobody manning it, but on the desk there was a big brass bell with a plunger device, so I banged it, hard. I was really worried, of course.

A door behind the desk opened and a large figure loomed out. I was astonished! It was my old navy mate, Ian Jones, large as life! He looked at me with equal astonishment. We both shouted together, 'Ben!'

'Ian!'

He rushed over to me as I rushed over to him. Hugged.

I said, 'Great to see you, Ian, I can't tell how great.'

Ian said, 'Fantastic to see you, Ben. Can't believe it. Why on earth didn't you ring and tell me you were coming?'

'I didn't expect you to be here, Ian. It was a surprise visit to see your parents, Ted and Mavis. I thought you could be anywhere in the world, doing your thing.'

'Finished with the Navy, Ben, bought myself out. Come into the office and I'll tell you all about it, mate. It's a sorry tale. You're the best thing that's happened for ages. I've got some brandy in the office. I could do with one, don't know about you.'

'Sure thing, Ian. I know something's wrong by the notice outside. Why on earth is the place for sale?' I was delighted, of course, that he had left the navy. Excellent news for me.

I followed him into the tiny office. He's another big guy, like me. Actually, I looked closely at him as I joined him. He is very like me in build and he has a craggy square sort of face, dark, with a big nose, much the same as me. Couldn't claim either of us have got film star faces!

I've got masses of curly black hair, and his hair is short and straight, though. When we both sat down, we sort of filled the room. A small window was wide open, thankfully. Ian reached into a cupboard and got out a bottle of brandy and a couple of glasses. He poured a generous measure into both. He looked at me fondly with his startlingly blue eyes (Mine are brown).

'Actually, the hotel has been sold,' Ian said, 'to a big chain of hotels called Best Western. They haven't taken the sign down yet. They take over at the end of this month.'

'But, why on earth…' I started.

'I tell you the whole sorry tale, Ben. Hang on while I have a good swallow of this golden nectar.' He took a long swig, so did I. Beautiful. French brandy.

He continued, 'The thing is, Ben, Dad's had a stroke. A really bad one, some months ago now. He had just finished one of his country songs, dressed in a cowboy costume, when he collapsed on our little corner stage. The ambulance came

44

really quickly and saved his life, but he has not recovered brain-wise.'

'He can't talk, nothing of sense; he needs 24-hour care, Ben. He can be aggressive and difficult to handle. Doesn't know me or Mum at all.'

Ian's eyes were wet. I couldn't believe what I was hearing. Ian's father, Ted, was a great bear of a man, full of energy and fun, a really lovely man and a great country singer, too. Dreadful news.

'So where is he, Ian?' I asked, I felt my own eyes becoming wet. Ted was like a second father to me. I'd now lost both of them.

'That's the other problem, Ben. He's in a private nursing home. It's superb but it costs the earth. That's where the money for the hotel is going, mate, to pay for his care. He is good, no other health problems, apart from his damaged brain, so he could live for many years. God knows what we'll do when the money runs out. It's a nightmare, Ben.'

'I suppose Mavis couldn't manage alone,' I said.

'No, no way, and even though I am now not in the service, I couldn't see myself running a hotel. I'm just not up for it, mate. It didn't bring in a lot of profit, you see, times are hard. Our country music was a big draw, sort of Welsh *Grand Ole Opry*, you know, and Dad was one of the main attractions. No, it wouldn't have paid for Dad's care, no way. Best Western gave us a good price.' He tailed off, gloomily.

I said nothing. We both had another draught of the brandy. God, it was lovely, the warmth seeping through my body, into my bones.

Ian gave me a half-smile. 'God, it's great to see you, Ben, fit and well. But, enough of my troubles, how are you doing, then? Your turn.'

So, I told him about my father's death, the kidnapping, my idea to turn myself into a PI, even about meeting Sue.

Ian had looked more and more shocked and dumbfounded listening to my story but grinned at the Sue bit. He had made no comments though, until I had finished.

Then he said, 'Gosh! Ben, and I thought I had problems! You've got more than me. But your Sue seems great. Look, I'm hungry, let's go to the local pub and have a meal, then you can come and meet Mum. She can't stand being in here in the hotel. Hasn't set foot in it since Dad's stroke, but she's strong; she's fine other than that.'

'Does not want to talk about Dad, really, but she's fine, and she'll be absolutely delighted to see you. Can you stay the night? I mean, at the B&B place we've rented in the town? It's nice and cosy. Stay for as long as you like, mate, you're not escaping any time soon.'

So that's what we did. The local pub food was great. We both had fish and chips and mushy peas, a huge meal fit for a king. The fish was fresh-caught and local. Really delicious. I've eaten lots of *haute cuisine* stuff, in top-class Michelin starred restaurants, but I'd swap any of them for fish and chips in a Welsh seaside resort! Any day of the week.

Chapter Seven

Ian and I swapped many tales over dinner and drank some Guinness, so it was with a warm glow inside that we strolled through the dark streets of Llandudno. It was not the holiday season yet, and the town was very quiet. Charming place, in my book, I was really enjoying myself.

This is the life. My favourite companion in my favourite place on God's earth. Brilliant.

It was only a few minutes' walk really. Up the hill. The views were amazing. Then Ian opened a gate in a hedge and motioned me to follow him through.

It was a typical Victorian seaside terrace, holiday B&B. *So this is what Ian's mum was turning her hand to now*, I thought. Mavis was great. I loved her to bits. She and Ted were a both great country acts. Mavis is small, busty and plump but squeezed into a corset and blonde wig she made a fair Dolly Parton tribute act too, as like a lot of small women she had a big voice!

She and Ted could sing, play guitars, tell jokes, some in Welsh, and were both really popular locally. As Ian had said, the hotel had a big reputation as a place for country fans to gather. They also booked other country musicians, some of them nationally known. The mention of *The Grand Ole Opry*, referred, of course, to the famous club in Nashville, Tennessee, home of country music.

Ted and Mavis had made several CDs, which sold well at the end of each concert, all covers, of course. *So all that has now finished* I thought, *sadly, as I followed Ian into his house.* He shouted for his mum, 'Look who's here, Mum!' and she came bustling out. She took one look and flew at me, giving me an enormous hug, and bursting into tears. I patted her back and made soothing noises.

'Oh, Ben, Ben, lovely it is to see you,' she said in her lilting Welsh voice, but choking and sobbing at the same time. 'All those country songs are so sad, and they've come true for us, love. I'll never sing them again, never.' It's true, of course, those country songs are nearly all about loss and pain, oddly enough.

I'm not really a fan. Music's not my thing. I like to read—mostly Military History stuff.

Ian said, 'Go into the lounge, Mum, Ben, I'll put the kettle on.'

I held Mavis' hand as we walked into the lounge and sat, next to each other on a couch. Mavis, I knew, was not just a singer, she was expert in the field of hospitality and had a degree in Hotel Management from Cardiff Uni. A really intelligent, charming lady. But I had never seen her so low.

Her husband, Ted, was worse than being dead. Still alive and fit and well in some ways, but a total stranger. Ian had told me that the last time she visited him, he had shouted nonsense words at her and tried to physically attack her. For some reason, she upset him and made him angry and violent.

So she had stopped going to see him at all. It really was tragic in the extreme. They had been such a loving couple.

48

Ted had been a wonderful host and entertainer, but it was Mavis that ran the business. Ted was never a brainy guy, more physical than academic, a real man's man.

We sat there, me still holding her hand, as she gradually calmed down. Ian brought in the tea and Mavis did the honours. She kept glancing at me as if reassuring herself that I was still there.

Ian said to her, 'Ben's been telling me what's been happening to him lately, since returning to his estate. His father has been killed in a riding accident, so Ben is now the Earl of Sumerton. But since he's been home, his brother's two children have been kidnapped, would you believe, but they paid a big ransom and the kids are back home and fine.'

'He's also met a girl he likes a lot and he's going to visit them on their ranch in Ireland. You won't believe who the girl is—she's the daughter of the rock god, Tony McGuire! So what do you think of all that, Mum?'

Mavis's eyes grew wide with astonishment. She had gasped several times as Ian's concise story about Ben unfolded. But it was obvious that the tale had made her feel a lot better. Her colour had returned and her eyes looked brighter. She gave a little laugh.

'Well, Ben, or should I now call you, *My Lord*, I've never heard anything like it, you really are an amazing man, and I'm just so grateful you are here. Ian's always talking about you, you know, and all the adventures you had in the Navy. You're both real heroes. And Tony McGuire, I love him. So handsome.'

'He's in the same class as Mick Jagger or David Bowie, that man. Gosh! *His daughter*, trust you! I hope you're not going to go away and leave us for another two or three years.

Please stay a while. Life seems so much better when you're here.'

I said that I would be staying for a few days' holiday, but I had to get back to work by the next weekend, and then I was going to Ireland for a couple of days but I would be back as soon as I could. I wanted to help. I had unlimited funds at my disposal and Ian is my best mate. I would not let him, or his family, down.

'Ah, now look that's very generous, Ben, but we couldn't accept money from you. Sorry, but I don't think that's the answer. We'll manage.' I secretly vowed to pay for his care, despite what his mum said. Second father. Give it time.

'Look, Mavis,' I said. 'I came down here with a second purpose. I want to bring those kidnappers to justice. The police can't help. We did not tell them about the kidnapping, just paid the money and got the kids back safe and sound. This is what families like ours always do.'

'But I'm determined to bring those bastards down one way or another and to do that I am going to open a business as a private investigator and I came down here to ask my best friend Ian to come and work with me, as a partner in the business. I will pay him a really good salary, because I know he is worth it.'

'As a SBS intelligence officer, he was the best around, and he is a genius regarding computers, IT and suchlike; any firm would give a lot to have him on the books. I'll pay him what he is worth—and that's an awful lot.' I kept glancing at Ian as I was talking to his mother, but his face did not reveal much. He just sat there and grinned at me, affectionately.

I said, 'Come on, Ian, it will be just like the old days in the Navy, you and me against the enemy! As Dickens' wrote:

"Such Larks, Pip, Such Larks!".' Ian's grin widened some more.

Ian said, 'Well, it really is too much to take in in one go. So I reckon we all need a night-cap. I'll go and fetch the brandy!'

Chapter Eight

That night, I slept in one of Mavis' four bedrooms, used for her new B&B trade. Ian lent me some clean clothes, pyjamas, underpants, socks, as I had brought nothing with me at all. I had not planned to stay overnight. He and I are much the same size. He had lots of pairs of jeans, tee-shirts, jackets, etc.

Mavis had spare toothbrushes, soap, towels, of course. So I was fine. It was all a novelty for me. A first. Earls' sons don't holiday in B&Bs!

When I say I slept, well it didn't come easy. My mind was a whirl—*Ted, Mavis, Ian, Kidnappers, Sue, Ted, Mavis, Ian, Kidnappers, Ted*…But eventually, sleep came and I had a good night. It was a very comfortable king-sized bed.

It was the sound of thunderous rain beating on my window that woke me up. It was pitch dark, but I managed to find my watch and looked at the time. 7.14.

There was a bedside light and, by feel and good luck, I found the switch and put it on. The room was en-suite, of course, so I had a good, long shower, which made me feel much more alive and ready to go.

I dressed in Ian's clean clothes and wandered downstairs. I had located the dining-room, so I went along there. Mavis greeted me warmly, giving me a hug and a kiss.

A full Welsh breakfast followed. Eggs, sausages, bacon, hash brown, fried tomatoes, beans, the lot. Lots of toast, marmalade, and good Welsh tea as well. It was really great. Mavis had no paying guests as the season had not started yet. Ian had joined me, a little later, but apart from the usual topic of Welsh weather, we said very little. Nor did Mavis.

I don't think any of us knew what to say. It would take time.

As far as the weather was concerned, the rain had stopped, and a weak, watery sun shone on Llandudno, and a brisk breeze blew in from the Irish Sea. I had wandered outside to smell the fresh, salty air, in the little front garden. Ian came and joined me. He was wearing a leather jacket, and he brought one for me, too, for which I was grateful. It was chilly, that breeze; bracing.

Ian had to go to his hotel. There were no guests but jobs still had to be done, post sorted and the telephone manned. There was always something to do, Ian said. I went with him, to have a chat, for something for me to do. I knew he had been thinking about my job offer but he so far had not broached the subject with me. I was quite content to wait.

The hotel had been opened very early by cleaning staff. Reduced in number at that time of year, of course. But still necessary. It was not a really big hotel as regards to number of bedrooms, but I knew it was a big job to keep clean, all the year around. We went into the office.

There was a small pile of mail to deal with, some electronic, but this did not take long, and I switched on the coffee maker and sat and read some old magazines. Soon, we were able to sit and chat. Soon, also, Ian brought up the subject of my job offer. I imagined he had spent a lot of hours of darkness thinking about it.

He sipped the coffee, then said, 'I have given a lot of thought to your suggestion about me coming to work for you as a private investigator. Of course, I am interested, and frankly excited about the idea. I had no idea what to do when the hotel is taken over by the new owners, which is, by the way, the end of this month. The hotel will be closed for several months while contractors do some refurbishment.'

'I thought I just would help Mum run her B&B, but she does not really need me, she has plenty of staff lined up for the busy times, all on short-term contracts. She is a tough, very intelligent lady, and will be fine. I probably would just be in the way, as I have the wrong skills entirely. If I could earn a good salary, like you offered, that would be really great, and I could help her financially.'

'I've only got my navy pension, generous as it is. But, Ben, I know absolutely nothing about being a PI you know! You'll have to tell me everything. Then I will do my best, that's about all I can offer you, mate.'

I laughed. 'Don't worry, Ian. Alright, I have surfed the Internet and read a couple of helpful books, but I really haven't much of a clue about starting up private investigation firms either, of course they are usually manned by ex-coppers. It will be "the blind leading the blind". But good fun and great to have you by my side, like the old days.'

'We'll get those bastard kidnappers as a first case. Maybe take on some real detectives, ex-coppers too, if we need to. No limit. So, do I take it you're in?'

Ian just shook my hand. His eyes were suspiciously wet.

I said, 'Look, can we go back and have a talk with your mum, she'll need to be kept in the loop, of course.'

'Sure, the cleaners will lock up when they finish, and anyway, it's not our hotel anymore, so let's go, boss!'

'Partner!'

'Yeah, boss.'

We both chuckled. I was really delighted.

'Oh,' I said. 'My name is now plain Mr Ben McGuire, PI, I've decided.'

'Mm. No comment, guv.'

We had another laugh. It was good.

When we arrived, Mavis had just started on making a cold ham salad lunch for us all. We sat her down to tell her the news, while the kettle boiled. Ian made the tea and left it to brew in the pot.

So I told her what Ian and I were going to do. She just nodded, happily.

Then I said, 'But your Ian and I actually have not got much of clue how to go about catching these kidnappers. Now, Mavis, you're cleverer than a box of monkeys, what do you think? Help us!'

Mavis smiled, indulgently. 'Flattery will get you everywhere, young man, but I know you mean well. What I would ask straight away is, why didn't you ask the police for help?'

'Families such as ours don't usually call in the police, Mavis. They really can't be of much help and they cause much unnecessary fuss. We have our own ways of dealing with matters, in most cases.'

'What you mean is the police don't get involved with super-rich aristocratic landowners, because they hate the sight of them.'

I laughed. 'Trust you to tell it as it is, Mavis, but you know our class tend not to use any of the public services, we have private education, private health care, etc., we pay through the nose for everything and yet we still have to pay huge sums in taxes, including inheritance tax, which has been the ruin of many.'

It was Mavis' turn to laugh mockingly. 'Oh, you poor old thing! I do feel so *sorry* for you. Anyway, my next question is, why are you going to all this trouble to find and punish these nasty kidnappers? Is it simply revenge, or what?'

'Yes. As usual, you have gone to the heart of the matter. These bastards have hurt me and my family. I want to hurt them back, make them pay.'

Mavis was silent for a while, thinking.

Then she said, 'Look, Ben, it's not your thing, catching kidnappers, so if I were you, I would hire myself a real private investigator, the best one you can find, and let him do the job for you. If and when he finds the crooks, you can take your revenge, I suppose, if that is what you want to do, though I can't condone violence.'

I suppose my glum face told her what I thought of her idea.

She laughingly continued, 'Alright. Look you, the other thing that struck me is that ransom money. You say it was in bitcoin, so I think this is a big organisation, not just some amateurs after your cash. If so, I would think that money can be traced. I have had a lot of experience of finance, running the hotel, and I don't think it is possible to totally hide the money trace completely.'

'My Ian is a genius with computers, no-one better at hacking or whatever Navy Intelligence needed to do, when he was in the service, weren't you, Ian? Have you still got the banking references they sent to your brother and his wife?'

I nodded.

Ian said, enthusiastically, 'That's a great idea, Mum! I would need to talk to some of my old mates in the navy, I'm sure they will let me log on to some of the supercomputers they've got. Couldn't do it on a PC, but *they* might be able to. I could call in a few favours, I reckon.'

Mavis smiled, lovingly. 'If you could hack into those kidnappers' systems, you could put in a bug and wipe all their accounts for them, or steal all their money. *That would be sufficient revenge*, I would have thought. After all, they did not use violence on your nephews, you said they were very well treated. Also, this way those criminals would not know who had done for them, so no reprisals.'

Both Ian and I looked at Mavis in awe. God, she's a clever lady, that.

I said, 'Wow, that's wonderful! But, Mavis, my instinct still is to wage violent warfare on those bastards, but I hear what you say. I promise to give your ideas a lot of thought. I really do want to be a PI, though, with Ian, who shares my enthusiasm for the idea. We'll have a great time together.'

Mavis threw up her hands in mock despair, 'MEN!'

We all laughed.

Chapter Nine

When I act, I act fast, as did Ian; it was the way we had been trained. I hired people to help me set up a business as a private investigator. I hired some office space in a brand-new suite of offices just built in Morecombe, with a good view of the bay. I consulted with lawyers and financial experts to ensure the business was legal. Ian sorted out the computers, of course.

Within a week, Ian and I had set the whole thing up. The company name, we decided, was B&I (Private Investigators) Ltd. Ben and Ian, of course, but I was now named as plain Mr Ben McGuire on the company records.

The next step was to hire a secretary. Ian left that job to me, as he was now busy trying to follow that money trail, which meant him travelling to Portsmouth to Navy HQ Intelligence services. Ian had been the best hacker in the force and had accessed accounts before that seemed impossible to hack, so we were lucky there.

As it happened, since retiring, he had already been called in, several times, to help on particularly difficult hacking jobs, so the team at HQ had no problem in assisting him.

I consulted our human resources lot, on our estate, and they guided me in the process of selecting staff. Damn complicated! I won't bore you with the details. However, I did my best and after a couple of young and not-so-young applicants submitted their CVs, I then, rather desperately, chose a short list and settled down in my new office to do some interviewing. Little did I know, at that time, what a monumental decision this was going to be.

I think it was the third candidate that caught my eye. A young lady, very attractive, tall, willowy and fiercely intelligent. Her name was Pat Lenton. I sat her down with me on the two modern chairs facing my desk, with a coffee table between us, and poured a coffee for each of us. It was permanently brewed in a rather sophisticated machine on a side wall.

The office was large, beautifully furnished, with huge windows showing a fine view of Morecombe Bay. The sun was streaming in. Pat really was a gorgeous young woman and I immediately thought, *God, if she looks like she is suitable, it would be great to have her on the staff, she's going to really attract customers, surely.*

We just chatted amiably as I went through her CV with her. She was really an experienced receptionist, which was my main requirement, she having held down a job with another detective agency, but where the MD had been giving her unwanted attention. I wasn't surprised, but I sensed a warning there.

I told her about myself, and my new-found girlfriend, and about my partner, Ian, who to my knowledge had never seemed interested in the fair sex at all and I knew also that he was rather shy in female company. I also told her about our previous careers in the Royal Navy, where the female officers tended to be brilliant, tough, and lesbian, if anything.

She seemed reassured and laughed when I confessed that neither Ian nor myself were professional detectives, but hoped to learn on the job, so to speak. I said to her, as you are experienced working with detectives, and knowing the type of work, Ian and I would be desperately needing her help. In fact, I suggested, she could be a receptionist, secretary and detective rolled into one! We both had a good laugh.

She told me she would love that! So I hired her on the spot, promising her a big salary raise against her previous job. She volunteered to start work the very next day, which was a Wednesday. I confessed that at the moment the only job on our books was the finding of the kidnappers, and gave her a brief history, without any detail.

I said there would probably be very little to do at first, until we really got going. She asked some interesting questions, which I couldn't really answer, about the process of advertising our services. I quickly told her that would be her first task! She was delighted—a dream job for her.

So that was a job done. Sorted. We had our secretary/receptionist, we had our office, we were up and running. B&I (Private Investigators) Ltd was born! Very exciting time. Ian was due back to report on progress on that same day, so that would be the first step in what I imagined would be a long journey ahead.

I decided to fill in the details of my initial tale of the kidnappers, telling her that it had been my brother's kids that had been taken and answering her questions. I told her also about my partner, Ian, who was away in Portsmouth trying to trace the money our family had paid to get the kids back. She showed great concern about what had happened, of course.

The next day, Ian arrived, and I introduced him to Pat. I could see he was very taken with the girl, and I rather thought she was also attracted to him. A great start.

So to Ian's report, which was to myself and to Pat as well. I could see she would probably be a big help to us right from the start. She told me, sometime later, that she had really always wanted to be a detective herself, so it was a dream come true for her.

Ian said, 'I had a great time in Pompey, seeing some of the old crowd again, chatting about old times, you know the sort of thing. They are a brilliant lot of guys, men and women alike, and they were superb in helping me to do that money trace. I reckon those kidnappers would be amazed how easily we managed to get into their accounts, but we've had worse tasks with the Russians and Chinese I can tell you, folks.'

He paused and sipped his coffee. I looked at him rather impatiently.

I said, 'So…?'

Ian laughed. 'OK, OK, so what did I find out? Brass tacks. Right. *Well*, as I thought, *it wasn't a UK or a Swiss account. The Swiss have really cleaned up their act of late. No, again as* I thought, *it was a Nigerian company.*'

'Name?' I said, still impatient.

'Hang on, give me my moment of glory here, boss man! The Nigerians are, at this time, the main money-laundering country in the world. Illegally, of course, but the government turns a blind eye and is probably involved. All the aid our country sends disappears into pockets. It is simply bribe money. I just wanted to set the thing to rights, Ben.'

I had to grin, but I said again, 'NAME!' which made Pat giggle.

'Right oh, cap'n. The name of the company is—long pause—Sherwood Timber Corporation. It trades as a timber merchant in the capital city of Nigeria, which is?'

Pat furnished the answer, gleefully, 'Ajuba.'

I said, 'Never heard of it. I've docked in Lagos a few times, but that's about all I know about Nigeria.'

Ian said, looking shyly at the gorgeous female, 'Well done, Pat. I can see you are going to be a treasure to us to ex-sailors!'

Pat coloured slightly and smiled at the young man, which made him turn a bit pink as well. I could sense romance in the air.

I quickly said, 'Sherwood, hey? Presumably a reference to Sherwood Forest in Nottingham, as they say they are timber merchants. I suppose the MD's name isn't Robin Hood by any chance?'

I got a rather dutiful laugh at my rather feeble joke. But actually it turned out to be not that far off the truth, funnily enough.

Chapter Ten

As the next day was Friday, I told Ian and Pat that I would not be with them on the next day, so Ian would be left in charge. Pat knew what she had to do, starting work regarding advertising our services, as said. I suggested to Ian that he concentrate on working on a plan of how to proceed now we knew the source of the kidnappers' activities.

He had said, as his mum had suggested, he could easily put a bug in all their accounts and wipe their screens totally blank, or steal all their money, but I asked him to have a good think about this and whether he had any other, alternative ideas. I still rather fancied some violence, I must admit. They say future wars will be fought by robots and computers. Can't see much fun in that.

I was off to Ireland for the weekend, as previously arranged. Ian knew about this, of course, and I left him in charge of the office, as I was going to spend a few days meeting up with my new girlfriend, Sue, and her family, at their ranch near Dublin. To tell the truth, I was really excited and looking forward to spending some time with the lovely Sue.

So much so that I really did not want to think about kidnappers, Nigeria, whatever. Since meeting Sue, she was really dominating my thinking. I think I was almost at a point of giving the whole PI thing the elbow, and leave it all to Ian and Pat.

So I packed a few essentials for a weekend's holiday and booked a private air-taxi to take me to Dublin airport. Father could have bought a plane but he always said he'd rather hire than buy, and I felt the same. I was to ring Sue and tell her my ETA and she said she would collect me from there, so this is what happened and we were soon driving together through some country roads in Ireland.

Sue was chatting gaily to me on the journey, telling me about her mother and her four sisters. She told me that she was the eldest of the five, and that none of them were married so far, and that she herself had been accused of soon being an old maid! This rather worried me, but I made no comment.

Eventually, at the end of a long lane, we turned through a pair of gates into the McGuire ranch. It was patently obvious that there were stables and horses around as they could be seen appearing as we passed through a wooded area. A familiar-looking estate that I was well used to visiting in many country houses back in England.

The scenery was rather beautiful I noted. Ireland is a very attractive country of course, very green—The Emerald Isle, as it is known all over the world. Green largely because of the abundance of rain, but that day, it was bright and sunny, for which we were both grateful. As said, I had just spent a whole year living in Dublin, not too far away, so there were no surprises.

I was excited to be sitting next to that gorgeous female, though she looked very different from the last time I saw her, all dolled up for the Grand National horserace. This time, she was wearing a simple country outfit of tweed skirt and woollen jumper, in a soft green, I suppose inevitably, and her hair was tied back to a ponytail. She appeared to have applied no make-up at all, but what do I know?

Anyway, I knew she looked and smelled fresh and beautiful to me, and I rejoiced in thinking she wanted to be with me. My first real girlfriend and I fancied her like mad.

Sue said she couldn't wait to show me off to her mum and sisters, which again worried me a little. *Trapped, moi? If so, I rather liked it*, I thought…*All a very new experience and a bit frightening. Frightened? Me a big, tough sailor? Perish the thought!*

As we approached Sue's family home, we had to pass through a security gate and security fencing, cameras, lights, etc., and a guardhouse. A stern-looking guard waved us through, unsmiling. To tell the truth, I was grateful for this. I remember reading about the late Frank Sinatra's estate and the sign on the gates which read: "You better have a good reason to be here."

Plus another that read: "Trespassers will be shot." Still a touch of the Wild West over there, but after our experience with the kidnappers, I felt sympathy. Superstars like Sinatra and McGuire were and are constantly pestered by the paparazzi of the world, and now they even use remote-controlled pilotless drones to invade your privacy.

It can be an awful world for the top stars of stage and screen, it really can. A nightmare.

The house was rather a surprise. It was huge and built in an Arts and Crafts manner, with tall chimneys, bays, gables, big Georgian windows—a heady mix and really beautiful. It was surrounded by an area that looked like it contained a covered swimming pool, gym, tennis courts and a fine terrace with lots of comfy-looking seating.

I'd discovered, by a little research, that Tony was an accomplished artist as well as a fabulous musician, whose paintings sold for huge sums, as if he needed it! I really looked forward to meeting him. I learned that he had just got back home after touring the Far East, to huge acclaim. *Perhaps I could ask him about that*, I thought.

Tony, like the late John Lennon, was a man of peace, totally against war of any kind. Also a vegan, with all his estate environmentally sensitive. So, as a true-blue right-wing Tory myself, being true to my class, of course, I had to be careful. Some of Tony's blockbuster songs, like Lennon's or Dylan's, dealt with the theme of peace, the brotherhood of man and suchlike.

I am somewhat cynical of all those sorts of idealistic ideas. I have seen, on RN missions abroad, so much extreme poverty, evil, horrible conditions poor people had to bear in war-torn countries like Afghanistan and Syria. The greed and corruption of governments and dictators with no regard for their people.

Years of observing such things does something to your brain, no doubt. I didn't want to think about it, and I hoped Tony did not go on about it, knowing of my naval career. I also worried about the vegan thing.

So I was intending to keep very quiet about such things, politics, like rock music, not my thing at all. I can't imagine how different Tony and I were! Sue had been on her phone keeping her family up-to-date on our progress, with a lot of giggling, probably between her and her sisters, so as we neared the front of the house, a gang of people came out presumably to welcome us.

There was a very handsome man, instantly recognisable as the great Tony himself, a large matronly lady, plus a gaggle of four young girls, all with beaming smiles on their faces. I tried my best to put a big beaming smile on my face too, bit of an effort! Not my scene.

Sue became enveloped by hugs, of course. Her sisters kept stealing a glance my way and giggling away. Tony came over to me after cuddling his eldest daughter. God, the man was charm personified. He actually hugged me! His Irish accent was very strong.

I really don't know what he said to me, but it was basically was to come and "sit myself down and tell me all about yourself" type of thing. Next came Dee, Tony's wife— another crushing hug—followed by all four sisters. I kept, somehow, the big beaming smile pasted on my face, but inside I was suffering.

I stammered something or other about "really looking forward to meeting them all and spending a weekend getting to know you" that type of thing, and eventually, I found myself sitting with a drink in my hand on a sunny patio being swamped with questions about myself, especially from Dee. I suppose mothers like to vet the men their daughters bring home.

Hoping for her child to settle down nicely and marry well, have a family, and provide lots of grandchildren for her to hug!

Somehow I survived, things calmed down a bit, as they eventually always do, and I started to relax. Tony then took me on a tour of his house and the estate. He especially wanted to show me his model train layout. Actually, I admit to being impressed, as it was huge, electronic, and amazingly complex and Tony had built the whole thing himself and spent most of his time at home fiddling with it.

He never mentioned his music at all, nor did he pry into my business. I found I really liked the man and I hoped he similarly liked me. He was, I suppose, a man's man, like me in essence. He certainly had the gift of the gab, hardly ever needing me to say anything at all. That's the way I like it. Less effort.

The weekend, like all such weekends, passed by in a blur and then it was time to leave. At least, the ice had been well broken. I'd met her folk. I suppose I now had to invite her to meet my brother and his wife. Mmm. *Courtship* I think they call it.

I knew I was lost. But I rather liked it. Or most of it. Especially the bed bit, I suppose. She really was amazing in bed!

Oh, by the way, they were not all vegan, including Sue, thank God.

Chapter Eleven

On the trip back to England, I passed the time away thinking about the kidnappers' problem. I had to acknowledge, to myself that now I had Sue to think about, the notion of bringing those bastards to justice had faded a lot. *I had to prioritise things*, I thought. Going after the kidnappers would inevitably mean that Sue would be in danger and I couldn't risk that now.

I needed time to sort things out. More time. Then I came up with a temporary solution. When next I was in our new office, I would discuss this idea with him. I could be very persuasive when I tried.

So, the next morning, in the office, I called our first meeting. Ever! We had a bit of a laugh about that. I had practiced what I would say to Ian and to Pat many times, tossing and turning in bed.

Pat had her notebook ready, actually it was a MacBook computer. Smart girl, that.

I said, 'I've been giving some thought to our first and only case, finding out who the kidnappers were and then bringing them to justice, one way or another.' Ian and Pat nodded their heads.

I continued, 'Ian, you have done a remarkable job in finding out the name of the firm, and its address, and you have suggested putting a bug in their accounts system to either wipe them blank, or to appropriate all their funds. Now, while I think this is an excellent idea in essence, I am not totally in agreement at this time.'

Pat looked me straight in the eyes and said, 'So...?'

Ian nodded in agreement with Pat, looking at her with adoring eyes, I thought.

He said, 'Yes, Ben, as Pat says, so what do you want us to do? You're the boss.'

'Right. Fair enough. What I've decided is that I want you, Ian, to go to Nigeria, to Ajuba, and investigate the firm that you have found, er, what was it? Oh yes, Sherwood Timber Merchants. I want to know all about them, and about their activities. At this time, we know nothing about them apart from the fact that the money our family paid went into their accounts.'

'I want to know how big this operation of theirs is, how widespread, what they do with the money, etc., everything you can find. Then write me up a report, like you have done many, many times for Naval Intelligence, and recommend what action we should take appropriately. I just do not have the time to go with you, Ian, as I'm tied up with running the estate and can't take more than two or three days leave at a time.'

'So you will be on your own. Pat will have to run the office solo while you are away.'

Ian nodded his head, thoughtfully.

He said, 'The idea rather occurred to me also, Ben. We need a lot more information about these buggers so that we can do a proper job on them. How long can I have over there?'

'Take as long as necessary, Ian, and enjoy yourself too. You are a top executive as far as status is concerned, so book in the best hotel in Ajuba, buy all the clothes, etc., you need for the trip. Money is no object, mate. Have a great time out there, you deserve it.'

'On that subject, I really must insist on paying for your father's nursing home fees—he was like a second father to me and I won't take no for an answer.' Ian started to say something, then subsided, he knew when he was beaten. I can be quite a force when I'm roused.

There followed a silence. Ian seemed lost in thought. Then he gathered himself together and grinned. I know he was really excited at the prospect of going to Nigeria. His face was a picture. Pat also looked pleased. I think she really liked Ian and rejoiced that he looked so delighted.

'What can I say, Ben? Thank you from the bottom of my heart. I will do as you say, of course I will.'

This was exactly what I hoped for. Time to think. The longer Ian spent investigating in Nigeria, the more time I had to sort things out in my mind.

Ian said, 'I'll get on to it right away, Ben, and thanks for the opportunity. I think that before I go, we should sit down and talk it all through in detail. An op like this needs a lot of preparation, as you well know, Ben. While I'm there, I will give you a ring every day to discuss progress of course and to keep you in the loop.'

I said, 'Look, Ian, you are much better than I at this sort of thing. So I think you should take the lead. Go and have a good think for the rest of today and see if you can come up with a plan of action, which we can discuss tomorrow. Pat, will you sort out the travel arrangements with Ian, and help him with the work of booking flights to Nigeria, etc., etc., all first-class travel, no queues, VIP stuff.'

'I'll help with this because that's the style I always travel anyway, as you probably imagine.'

Pat said, 'Look, Ian, I think you should use a false name and address, we don't know how much this criminal gang knows about us—they might know your name and your association with Ben.'

I said, 'That's good thinking, Pat. Ian, perhaps you can call in a few more favours from your old colleagues in Navy Intelligence to provide you with a cover, like we often did over the years.'

Ian looked at Pat again with obvious adoration. 'Yes, I will sort that out, Pat, best to be careful, of course. We don't know anything about these kidnappers, but it is obvious they are well-organised. I'll have to be careful, but don't worry too much, Pat, I'm well used to working under cover. I've done it dozens of times and never been unmasked.'

'There's always a first time,' she said, looking worried.

I said, 'Don't worry, Pat, Ian's the best in the business.'

Pat smiled, gratefully. She said, 'I think it's well time for some coffee and biscuits, folk.'

The rest of the day passed pleasantly enough. Pat continued on her task of advertising our presence, and I did some research into the work of a private investigator. I rather hoped that when we finally got started, the cases would not roll in too much, as they would probably be divorces, employment disputes, that sort of thing, rather than anything exciting, like the fictional PIs in the movies deal with so entertainingly.

The best sort of case that seemed to be on offer, in terms of my interest, was missing persons.

What my researches had revealed so far had not been very encouraging. Sadly, most of the work, according to the stuff I was reading, was in following errant husbands or wives, gathering divorce evidence. Ugh! But as it turned out, the first proper case we accepted was rather more interesting…

Chapter Twelve

I need to start this report with a bit of background information about this country, known as "The Giant of Africa".

This is an amazing place. It really is. English is spoken everywhere, as it is the national language, due to fact that it used to be an English colony, of course. But, in spite of that, there are some five hundred other languages spoken here by the same number of ethnic groups or tribes.

It is still very much a tribal country. Would you believe there are over 186 million Nigerians living here, three times the population of the UK. Half of these are of the Christian faith. Most of the rest are Muslims, but there are lots and lots of other faiths, too.

I'll deal with what I reckon are the good things first, Ben, Glenda. Nigeria is fully democratic, and the elections really are fair. As the name "Giant of Africa" suggests, it is an emergent huge force in the economy of the world, largely because of the vast petroleum resources here. Ajuba is a modern city, as good as any European or American city, really beautiful to look at, and the streets are safe to walk around, safer than most other cities of the world.

It really is a good place to live and I've enjoyed my time here in this fine, civilised city.

Now for the not so good things. Human rights here are, frankly, appalling. Rape, torture—all the obscenities you can name—are endemic here. The law is medieval. Brutal. Minor crimes, like "drunk and disorderly" are punished ruthlessly and without mercy. Homosexuality is unlawful and punished dreadfully. Policing policy is strictly zero tolerance.

On the other hand, child abuse, child labour, racial discrimination—these are common and largely ignored by the authorities. The vast numbers of the poor are treated very badly, they have nothing. Many people are starving and just about existing, living in dreadful, squalid shacks and with very little help, despite this being such a rich country.

AIDS and other diseases are prolific, with no real health service at all. Dreadful. Really sad. I was appalled, travelling about. I felt like an alien. I felt ashamed, too, to be a rich tourist. How can we treat human beings like this?

Finally, I must mention that kidnapping is common. You might have heard of the Muslim terrorist gangs, Boko Haran? Kidnapping schoolgirls? Crazy.

Anyway, enough background stuff. I've left it to the end of my stay to write about such general info. What follows is from my daily notes taken at the end of each day.

Day One

I must say I have enjoyed the travel here, in luxurious comfort, thanks to your bank balance, Ben! Also, the hotel is the last word in modern accommodation, absolutely wonderful to an ordinary Welsh sailor. Fantastic. I have wandered about the nearby area, which is very nice, clean and greenery everywhere, looking quite exotic.

In the near distance is a huge cliff, or hill of some sort, must be thousands of feet high. Really impressive. I've asked and I've found out it is called the Zuma Rock. I have just spent the day accustoming myself to this city and enjoying all this luxury. The food, incidentally, is fabulous.

I did ring you both and tell you all this anyway. Tomorrow the real work starts. I decided, as you know, not to ring you every day, as originally promised, but to only ring when there is something interesting to report.

Day Two

Last night, I talked to some of the other guests at this hotel. They were nearly all male and were Americans, Germans, and Russians mostly, and I think all employed or connected to the oil industry here, overhearing some conversations. It got very noisy at times, with a lot of very loud laughter.

I met a middle-aged American guy at the bar. We both ordered whisky, though his was bourbon and mine scotch. I had a brief conversation with him about the merits of the two whiskies, and then managed to ask him whether he had heard of a firm called Sherwoods, but he looked blank.

He took me back to his noisy table to meet some of his friends and he kindly asked them all if they had heard of Sherwoods, with the same result, I'm afraid. This really wasn't surprising as it was a long shot by me, but it was a start, I suppose.

As you know, my cover here is that I'm an executive called David Roberts, in the field of export and import of goods. So far, I don't think anyone is watching me. I have been well-trained to spot such people, as you are, Ben. Nothing.

I took a taxi this morning to go and have a look at Sherwoods. It turned out to be a very ordinary-looking timber merchants' site, lots of large sheds, lots of stacked timber, etc., not open to the public, lorries going in and out, in an enormous business park to the North of the city. There did not appear to be a reception office, unfortunately, not that I intended to visit there in person.

There did not seem to be any point in doing that, I thought. I could hardly pretend to be connected to the timber industry, could I? It struck me that this was not going to be easy. I could see no way of infiltrating the company, which is our usual procedure. I might pass, physically, as a lumberjack, but really! A no-no, as the Americans say.

I was glad I hadn't wiped all their accounts, or stolen their money, so that was worthwhile. So well done, Ben!

I went from there to a city information office, rather like our tourist information offices. The taxi driver had taken me there and was willing to wait while I went in, but I sent him away with a large tip. He was a lovely man. All the local people I met had been friendly and helpful, I must say. Actually, it was quite good.

I found out a fair amount about Sherwoods there, as they had a lot of information about Ajuba companies on file. It certainly seemed to be a genuine timber and lumber business, plus building products related to timber. No doubt about that.

Nigeria has an awful lot of trees! They export timber all over the world.

So at least I'd found out it was a legitimate company, which was something. I called another taxi and went back to the hotel to consider my next step.

It had occurred to me that if Sherwoods were really robbing the rich to give to the poor, as their name vaguely suggests, however far-fetched, then I need to find out more about the poor. Were they getting money from Sherwoods? If so, how? At least it was something I could do, to justify this trip. Otherwise, it is a dead end.

I found out, by looking on the Internet about Sherwoods, that the owner and managing director of the firm was a German by the name of Hans Kruger, so not Robin Hood, Ben! I made some more enquiries about this man and it seems that he is a noted billionaire philanthropist, with fingers in many pies, so that was interesting.

I could not think any way to contact the man himself. Whether that would be worthwhile was another consideration. These people are well protected from busybodies like me, as you and I both know. I rather bet you, Ben, are not easy to contact yourself, are you, mate?

Day Three

Had a real stroke of luck! I was having a coffee after breakfast when a tall, thin man came and introduced himself to me, in Welsh! He said his name was Alain Parry. He had overheard me ordering breakfast and noted my Welsh accent. He asked the waiter about me, so he had decided to come and introduce himself as a fellow Welshman!

Birds of a feather, he said. So, we had a cosy chat in our native language, over coffee. I found out he was a doctor working for the charity Medicines Sans Frontiers helping in the fight against AIDS, principally amongst the poor. I suppose you have heard of MSF—in English, "Doctors Without Borders". Alain, or Doctor Alain, had a French mother and a Welsh father, also a doctor, which explained his Christian name, by the way.

Why this was a stroke of luck, of course, is that Alain was a fund of knowledge about the plight of "the poor" here in Nigeria, and about the curse of AIDS which had become widespread among the poor population here. I pretended I was simply a tourist and managed to invite myself to join him for a day or two to observe his daily routine, simply out of interest.

I thought that after getting to know him better, I might be able to ask him whether he knew, or could find out, whether a firm called Sherwood was a donor to MSF, without raising suspicion. Clever, or what?

I looked up MSF on the Internet that night and was amazed at the size of the organisation, founded by a small group of some remarkable French doctors who flew out, illegally, to the country of Biafra to give medical help to the millions of that countries' population starving to death at the time, when all her borders had been closed by the then crazy rulers of Nigeria.

Remember Biafra? Anyway, MSF was now a huge organisation with some 40,000 employees working in many oppressed countries around the world, setting up free hospitals and treating the poor. I was very impressed, I must say, and I really liked Alain, as well, and enjoyed his sparkling company. A really nice man and dedicated to his job.

After breakfast then, Alain and I went off, by a short train ride, then a taxi, to the free hospital where he works. It was set in the jungle. The taxi took us on dirt roads lined with shacks. It was suffocatingly hot and humid and there were clouds of flies, really nasty conditions.

Luckily, the taxi was air-conditioned, and we did not have to do much walking outdoors. Both Alain and I were well smeared with anti-insect cream of course.

The track up to the hospital was crowded with people, men, women, loads of children, including lots of babies, and they all looked happy, glad to be there. I imagine some of them had walked miles through jungle tracks; they were all covered in flies, which they ignored. I found it a sad sight. Did not really want to know.

The hospital, once we entered, was clean, modern, cool, and hardly any flies at all. It felt wonderful. It was just as crowded as outside, but the people must have thought they were in paradise. They all were smiling and laughing. Amazing.

Alain had to go and do his job, but before he went off, I asked him if he could find out whether Sherwoods were donors of MSF and he rang his office and asked them to do the honours, which was really nice of him. He told me they would find out the information and ring him back. I went off to find the hospital restaurant, where I was to meet Alain later on for a late lunch, free to all, by the way.

I spent the time chatting to the patients, who all spoke English of course. They were so happy! So grateful, almost embarrassingly so. It was really interesting talking to them and I found out a lot about them. They did not complain about how they lived; I imagine they were frightened to complain to a white stranger like me.

Lunch was really good actually. All vegetarian but delicious and, as said, free to all. I really like artisan African food. Alain told me he was spending the day giving anti-viral injections to AIDS victims, who numbered many thousands, if not millions. Most of the patients were suffering from undernourishment, chronic diarrhoea, poor hygiene, typical of the very poor all over the undeveloped world.

Then Alain's phone rang. He told me, would you believe, that Sherwood was a major donor to MSF and had *just given five million pounds to them!* Obviously, the result of your kidnapping ransom, Ben!

He was curious about why I had asked about a specific company like that and I mumbled a hastily-thought-up reason, which thankfully he seemed to accept, but he did give me a funny look. I can't blame him, really. Incredible news wasn't it. Makes you think.

I must tell you that during the afternoon, a seedy young local man kept pestering me about what he described as a "gorgeous young virgin" that he could provide for my amusement for very little money. He was very persistent. Eventually, I had to floor the bugger, which made me feel a lot better.

Really, Ben, Pat, that's it. End of my report. I don't think I'll gain anything from staying here any longer and I'll be glad to come home. It's up to you, Ben, what happens next. But I would always support Robin Hood, rather than the Sheriff of Nottingham! Sorry about that. One bottle of your two hundred pound champagne would feed some of these poor people for a year, mate. Crazy.

Ian

***

To tell the truth, I was relieved to get Ian's report. I no longer really wanted to exact revenge on those kidnappers. Don't get me wrong, such criminals cannot be condoned. They caused an innocent family, like ours, much harm. The main reason was Sue. She had changed everything for me. I no longer felt alone, just me against the world, so to speak.

I now had a good excuse to drop the whole thing. I really felt that MSF, as described in the report, deserved every penny of my ransom money. I vowed to myself that I would make an annual donation to them. To salve my conscience maybe. But I can't take on the worries of the world.

Rich people like me do a lot of good too, keeping the wheels of industry turning, providing lots of jobs, investing in new ideas, etc., etc., etc. We pay millions of pounds in tax into the public exchequer.

Think of Virgin Industries—Richard Branson is really the good face of the very rich? Well, I think so. Not inherited, dubiously-sourced wealth, like ours. He came up from nothing. A wonderful entrepreneur. The nation really needs these guys, and dolls, of course. We'd have not had railways, airplanes, etc., without rich folk investing in them in the first place, risking their capital.

End of rant. On with the story.

Chapter Thirteen

With our first case closed, our new enterprise of B&I (Private Investigators) Ltd was set to go. All that we needed was some cases. Pat had done a wonderful job of advertising our presence in the market and we waited for all her hard work to bear fruit.

We didn't have to wait long. A woman rang our bell. Pat buzzed her in. She was a large and imposing lady, with an upper-class accent to rival mine. She swept in and demanded to see our "best detective" at once. I happened to be in our reception area talking to Pat at the time, so I approached her and asked her to come with me into my office.

This was my first mistake! I should have left it to Pat to sort her out.

The lady snorted, 'So you are the best detective, are you? I insist on having the best.'

I replied, 'Madam, I am the owner of this agency. How may I help you?'

'Right! I want you to find my Wilfred. He has disappeared.'

'Wilfred—your husband, your son…?'

'He is a Corgi, you stupid man!' She shouted, contemptuously.

She then told me, at long length, all about her beloved dog, virtually from its birth, with no sparing of details. She punctuated her tale with "and er's" giving me no opportunity to break into her narrative. It seemed like hours before I could stop her flow long enough to tell her, firmly, that we did not find missing dogs, suggesting to her disgust that she ring her local dogs' home.

It still took some time to convince her that we would not help her. She offered a lot of money, but eventually, I persuaded her to leave, which she did, in a huff! I was exhausted. I'd rather fight a dozen armed terrorists!

Never again! I at least now knew the value of a good receptionist who would act as a filter to get rid of the unwanted clients. So something gained. I soon found Pat was worth her weight in gold. Could not do without her. She told me that lots of weirdos called either on the phone or in person, with fantastic tales including being abducted by aliens. She was used to that sort of thing from her previous employment, thankfully.

I, of course, could actually not spend much time at the agency, as I had to return to run my estate. I could not just leave everything to Charles, even though he had not complained at all. So I was soon back in harness, and at least now I could manage, with a lot of help and advice, to take up the reins and do a reasonably good job of being chairman of the main board.

In that capacity, I had to spend a lot of time visiting the various companies we headed, listening to grievances and suggestions, and just showing my face. It wasn't too bad and I enjoyed meeting a lot of my employees in that manner. Lots of toadies, of course! But hey! Toadies are a comfort.

So I left the agency in the capable hands of Ian and Pat, asking them to ring me if there was a problem. I told them that if a suitable case came along, take it and see how it went. They were quite happy to make a start. I know they both really liked spending time together and made a great team. I rather envied them.

As for Sue, we had come to an arrangement. I had found out, while I was with her at that weekend in Ireland, that she was in fact, the owner and managing director of her own company, a firm of architects. She was fully qualified as an architect herself and loved every minute of it, so during the working week, she would run her company and I would run my estate, and then most weekends, hopefully, we would meet up either here in England or in Ireland.

Now, I could not impose myself, and Sue, on my brother much longer, so I had to look for some suitable accommodation to live in.

Incidentally, on the subject of houses, Sue had excitedly told me that she was designing a family home for herself which would be in the grounds of her daddy's estate, as she put it. There were lots of room, of course, it was a big estate. She was intending to move into this house "when she got married, settled down and had a family"—more hints at me, of course.

I, wisely, made no comment. I was not ready for marriage and kids. No way! Years away. But I would hate to lose Sue, so it was a real problem. I tried to put it out of my mind. Sue had said, that at twenty-nine years old, her sisters had teased her that she was "an old maid". Another hint! Pressure. And did I want to live on her daddy's estate for the rest of my life? In Ireland? What about my estate? Big problem.

I got one of my staff to find me a suitable house. I needed something pretty large, with a garden, if I was to invite Sue over for a weekend, and maybe Tony or other members of her family. Another problem loomed. How would I cope with being the genial host, especially if the international star, Tony McGuire came along and needed entertaining?

I would need staff, that I was clear about—cook, housekeeper, gardeners, cleaners. My God! What had I let myself in for?

The secretary I trusted with the job of sorting all this out for me was marvellous. In seemingly no time at all, she told me she had found something that I might like and offered to drive me to see it and possibly approve hiring it for a year or so.

So the next morning, bright and early, found me sitting by this girl, a Kylie Reynolds by name, in her Honda car and speeding at a stunning pace down country roads a few miles away from Morecombe, but on the coast. Kylie was one of many office staff we employed at the estate's head office; a small and plump girl with a serious manner and owl-like spectacles.

Quite frighteningly clever, too. There's no doubt, like in the RN, it's the other ranks that really run the show, while officers basically did what they were advised to do. Not fair at all.

We drew up outside a relatively small manor-house type of thing. Red brick, probably Victorian. All very nice and tidy. Kylie rang the bell and then introduced a very pleasant middle-aged couple to me, housekeeper/butler. I was told the previous tenants had moved to Australia to be with their daughter who lived over there.

The staff had all had their employment terminated but would stay on if I wanted them. I had a quick look around and really, it was perfect. It was fully furnished, in a really nice, cosy country-house style. I decided to take it on, lock, staff and barrel. Job done.

I can't tell you how relieved I was! As Kylie, still with a serious face, drove me back to the office, I told her how much I appreciated what she had done for me. She made little comment. Even when I told her that there would be a substantial bonus for her at the end of the month. Just a calm, 'Thank you, Sir.'

Amazing. I wondered if she ever smiled. Fantastic member of staff. So damned efficient, it made me feel inadequate. I hope that girl goes far, she certainly deserves it and I will make my feelings known to the management, I determined.

I went back to my brother's home and told them the news. Although, they protested, I think they were secretly pleased to have the place back just to themselves. So I moved in to my new house, on a five-year lease/hire. It was strange at first being on my own, even though I had been on my own in Ireland, and indeed ever since my injury and retirement.

It still seemed a bit lonely. But the couple running the place for me were great. We got on well. Mr and Mrs Croston made me very comfortable indeed and Annie Croston was a great cook. Each day, she came to me and asked what I would like for breakfast, lunch and supper. I soon settled down and began to enjoy myself.

I was due in Dublin the coming weekend, Tony was off touring in Japan or somewhere, with his wife, and the sisters were at college, or school, or uni, whatever. So it would be just Sue and myself. I really looked forward to a lot of great sex, plus going out and having a good time, just the two of us. And, for once, it turned out to be as good as it gets, as they say. Absolute Heaven.

But I realised I was in it now for the long game, no turning back. Even marriage seemed to be at least a possibility, one day…Was I weakening? I don't know. Scared? Yes.

Chapter Fourteen

The weather was becoming really hot for the UK. It was June, "flaming" as it sometimes, rarely, does. I don't like hot weather very much at all, so I was suffering a bit. I was due a holiday but Sue was unable to join me at the time, so I decided to stay at home for a few days, then maybe go somewhere abroad, that was cooler, perhaps. Alaska.

The agency was going along well, with Ian and Pat really learning the ropes fast, so I was not needed there. To tell the truth, I was not now really looking forward to doing the great detective bit. Sitting in a car, "observing", or following people. I'm not an easy person to hide away, too big.

I told Ian that if a really interesting case came along, I'd be happy to help out, but divorces, that sort of thing, I didn't really have the stomach for. Ian was quite happy. He was with the girl he was falling in love with, he had a good job and was earning a lot of money that he could send to his mum and save for rainy days ahead, with his poor father.

The agency was already making a small profit, so that was good news. It was all working out fine. It wouldn't last.

It was a Sunday. Sue had got a family celebration to attend, so we were not together this time. I had breakfast and wondered how to spend the day which rather loomed ahead. I made a quick, and as it turned out, rather foolish decision. I would go for a long walk in the local hills. As said, the weather was blisteringly hot and humid.

Mrs Croston made me a small picnic and found my backpack for me. *She also packed a bottle of spring water What more do I need?* I thought. *I'm a big tough sailor*, I thought. No problem, then.

I headed for the hills, dressed in tee shirt and shorts and an old pair of trainers. I started off at a run and thoroughly enjoyed the exercise. The countryside was remote for England, no obvious landmarks in sight, just field after field after field and narrow country roads. Great.

I am not noted for my navigational skills, as my old Navy colleagues would tell you. In fact, I am pretty useless in that skill, relying entirely on satellites, but as one of my pals had said to me, 'If you have never been lost, you've led a sad life.'

I must have run six or seven miles in about an hour and had not seen another living soul or any traffic. It was really hot, and sort of airless. I knew I was totally lost already, as the roads were complex, with many tee-junctions. I had always turned right at each one of these, which was something.

I imagined this would eventually mean I would be back where I started, but somehow this had not happened. I stopped under a tree, sat in the shade, and drank half my water in one gulp, which was not a good idea, in retrospect. I was soaked in sweat. I told myself that I had gone out for the day and a day I should do, whatever happened. So after cooling down a little, I got to my feet and walked, rather than ran.

In a few minutes, the lane crossed over a tiny stream, so I was able to fill up my bottle of water, which was good. Actually, I had walked over what appeared to be an ancient pack-horse bridge. On the other side, the ground opened up and it appeared that the field was common land, so I left the lane and started walking across the field.

I came to a 5-barred gate, vaulted over it, walked up a grassy slope covered in wild flowers, very nice, but what was not so nice was that there now appeared billions of midges, all biting away merrily. I imagined that it was because of the little stream. I wished I had brought a hat.

I continued climbing and soon reached the summit of the hill and the view was quite stunning. I was basically in the foothills of the mighty Pennine Range, where there were peaks, as I knew, rising to two thousand feet and more, covered in ice and snow in the winter, but as it was June, they looked green and inviting. I must confess now that I had not brought my phone, I rarely carry a phone, as said.

I did not want anyone phoning me from the estate, of course. I also had no watch, and no money. This was deliberate, but, I suppose, rather foolish of me. I wanted an adventure, and now it appeared I'd got one! The challenge was—find my way home. No prob.

I looked carefully at that stunning view and tried to get my bearings. The sun was right overhead and no help at all. I could see fields, hedges, trees, and nothing else, except, in the far distance, a church steeple. Clever me thought that where there was a church, there would be a village, maybe a pub, civilisation. So I tried to take a bearing on that steeple.

I wished I had a compass! Anyway, I started walking in the general direction of that church, more in hope than expectation. I was still quite happy at that point, not really worried at all. What was the worst that could happen? I'm a big, tough, sailor, I told myself for the umpteenth time. It was fine. If I keep moving, something will turn up eventually, after all I'm in England, not the Sahara Desert!

I stopped, ate my sandwiches, drank some water, then started off again, refreshed. Billions of flowers, daisies, clover, buttercups surrounded me as I bounded down the slope on the other side of the hill, and another billion or so insects accompanied me too, all biting me continually.

The hill became really steep and rocky and so my progress became almost like flying, at a furious pace, trying to outrun those midges and failing miserably, of course.

Now I come to the strange part of my tale. I've told this tale many times since, and I don't think anyone believed me, but I assure you what follows really happened. Honest. I'm a practical, down-to-earth guy, not given to flights of fancy and I will admit, I was feeling a bit light-headed, with the sun beating down on my unprotected head and I think some folk think that I must have had "a touch of the sun" that afternoon. I'll leave you to judge.

It became suddenly deathly quiet. If you listen carefully when in the country, there are lots of sounds—birds, insects, the wind, not necessarily in the willows, farming noises, animals, cows, sheep, dogs barking. It certainly is not totally quiet, like it became that afternoon. A spooky sort of stillness in the air. The insects had gone away, and the only sound came from the passage of my feet on the ground.

After descending further down the grass slope, I came upon a boundary wall made of stones, dry stone walling about five feet tall. I clambered over this and down a triangular field, down, down, and at the end of this was another boundary wall, and, sort of suddenly appearing, a farm house or cottage of some kind, with limewashed stone walls, small windows with white curtains pulled back.

It was the back of the cottage of course. There also looked like a large barn, also constructed of stones, but not limewashed, just grey stones. Both buildings had slate roofs topped with red terracotta ridge tiles. Attractive.

I approached the farm with extreme caution. I half expected to be confronted at any minute by a red-faced angry farmer with a shotgun pointing at me. I couldn't blame him, I must have looked like a homeless tramp myself!

But it was all quiet. I skirted slowly around to the front of the farm cottage. It was really a very attractive cottage, with a deep porch, a cottage garden in full bloom, and a well, complete with an oak bucket on a chain.

I knocked on the door of the cottage. Nothing, not a sound from within. I knocked again, really hard. Nothing. So I made a bee-line over to the well. I peered down into the depths and there was obviously water at the bottom, some twenty feet or so down.

I removed a wedge from the gearing and wound the bucket down to the bottom, pulled it up and tasted the clear water. It was delicious! There was an iron ladle and an iron cup, which I filled and had a long drink.

Next thing was, I felt a severe blow to the back of my head and then I was pushed forward and found myself falling, falling, falling. I lost consciousness for a minute or two. Then I woke up and I was standing in the water, which came up to my neck. My head was paining like mad. I looked up and saw what looked like a Chinese man staring down at me.

I was astonished. It was like a dream. I thought I would wake up soon. But the pain at the back of my head, and cuts and grazes on my arms and legs were real enough. I was a mass of pain. I thought to myself, *I have been in some pretty hairy fixes several times in my career, but this one is the worst of the lot. What the hell could I do?*

On the other hand, I was alive and kicking, which of itself was remarkable as I'd obviously fallen a long way down. The water must have saved my life. I must have entered the water unconscious and headfirst, I thought, and then had a strange memory about the day I went to a local fete and watched a man dive from a high tower into a barrel of water and emerged, smiling and triumphant, acknowledging the applause of the audience crowded around.

I must have been lucky. Very lucky.

My training took over and I assessed the problem I had, logically. The well was about five feet in diameter. I am over six feet tall and have had some mountaineering training, part of the SBS course. I tried to wedge myself across the well and managed to do this fairly easily. I took a step upwards, and then another. Pushed down with my arms underneath me.

I slowly began to move upwards. I rested a while, then started walking upwards again, remembering doing such a move while mountaineering, under training in Finland. It really was quite easy to do. I was lucky again, the walls were of stone, with lots of crevices and ledges. In a remarkably short time, I reached the top.

Now I had to get out without falling down again. I grabbed the bucket and thankfully the wedge in the gear to it held firm. With a supreme effort, I levered myself over the edge of the well and collapsed in a heap on the ground. There was no sign of a Chinaman, thank God. I was a sea of pain. Shattered. But happy to have survived and on dry land in the hot sun. I closed my eyes and I think I lost consciousness again.

The next thing that happened was that I heard a woman's voice, in rather cultured tones, asking me whether I was alright. I opened my eyes. She was lovely. She looked like she was an actress in a Jane Austen drama, poke bonnet, long white cotton dress. I wondered if I had died.

This girl, she was young enough to be called a girl, rather than a woman, offered me a drink of water. She had a little girl with her, very pretty, also with a bonnet on her head, but with a shorter white dress. She had huge green eyes and was clutching the older girl's dress and peering at me shyly from behind it.

I thanked her and tried to stand up but found it very difficult.

'I have had an accident,' I said, rather croakily. I really did feel awful.

'Look, Sir, wait here. I'll fetch my pony and trap, and drive you home.' The little girl tried to pull her mother, or older sister, whatever, away. She obviously wanted to go somewhere, away from the floundering tramp-like monster, that was me.

I don't remember much after that. But Charles and Nancy told me they found me knocking at their door, in an awful state, they had called an ambulance and had me carted off the hospital. They did not see a pony and trap, or a girl and a child in old-fashioned clothing. Just me, unfortunately.

I was in hospital for several days recovering. The doctor I saw said I was lucky that I had not suffered any serious damage, just cuts and bruises, mild concussion and shock.

The blow to my head had landed on a titanium implant in my skull. Lucky, again. Saved my life.

Now you must feel that was a strange enough story, but it got stranger. Try as I might, I could not find the cottage with the well in front. I must have covered the local area with a toothcomb, so to speak, but there was no sign of it anywhere and nobody local had ever heard of such a farm as I described. Had I travelled back in time, hundreds of years?

Nonsense, surely. The doctor in the hospital reckoned I had slipped when leaping down the hill and had tumbled down to a stream, hitting several rocks on the way down. I dismissed this theory as rubbish. How did I get home, then, I reasoned? I could not have walked all that way in that state.

So, there it was. That's a true story. If it was just a dream, why was I so injured? I had obviously been hit violently on the back of my head. I was quite badly hurt. How else could it have happened? The truth was that I had been attacked and thrown down a well, as I have described.

But, where? And what about that Chinaman? Those kidnappers? Was he the guy who had paid those two scouser thugs? Had he been following me?

I'll leave you to judge. Enough. Back to the main story.

Chapter Fifteen

It was a relief to go back to the agency and I looked forward to spending some time being a detective. Ian had said they had a client coming who sounded like he had an interesting case for us. He and Pat had already handled a couple of cases with success, with Pat really leading the way. *It was time for me to make a real effort*, I thought.

I confess to feeling nervous and rather a fraud. It was to be my first case, and I really would be feeling and bluffing my way as we go along. *If Ian and I were to make fools of ourselves and make a mess of the case, we really might have to think again about the whole thing*, I thought.

The client duly arrived and was shown to my office by Pat. I had asked that Ian joined me and so I had to do the introductions before we started. His named was Alan Wilkinson and he said he was the owner and chairman of the eponymous firm of printers and stationers in the town, employing, he said proudly, 200 staff.

'How can we help?' I asked.

Mr Wilkinson looked embarrassed, but he had a clear, firm voice and he looked fit and capable. He wore a blue suit, white shirt and striped tie, all immaculate and he appeared to have a somewhat commanding presence, helped by a large, hooked nose and penetrating, unblinking, grey eyes.

He looked at both Ian and I appraisingly and seemed satisfied with what he saw. He probably thought we looked like ex-coppers.

'Look,' he said, 'it is a family matter regarding my only child, my daughter, Megan. She is nineteen and attending Manchester University on a degree course in Politics and Economics. But, before going any further, I would like to know your fee structure.'

I nodded and reached into a drawer in my desk and brought out our glossy flyer detailing our costs and fees for professional services rendered. I said, 'We do not charge anything in advance. If we take on your case, we will give you a full breakdown of our fees and costs on a week-to-week basis. If we do not satisfy your requirements, there will be no fees, just costs to pay.'

Mr Wilkinson made no comment, he just continued to read our flyer for a minute or two, then he looked up and smiled, lighting up his handsome face.

'It all seems fair to me, but I must caution you, I am nobody's fool when it comes to business and I shall expect excellent service at all times. I have never had recourse to use private investigators before, but to tell you the truth, I'm really worried about my Megan. She…' He suddenly broke off, his voice breaking, he looked really emotional, eyes brimming with tears.

'Go on,' I said, softly.

He took a deep breath, blew his nose, then continued, 'Megan's mother left me several years ago—I don't really blame her now—but she left me for one of my reps. For a reason I do not quite understand, she left Megan with me. Megan was only fifteen at the time, but she had become sulky and disobedient to Jill, my wife, you know how teenage girls become.'

'She and her mum were no longer speaking to each other. Megan wanted to stay with me because she could twist me around her little finger. I really doted on her and she knew it, of course.'

Neither Ian nor I made any comment. We both just tried to look "understanding". We knew nothing of teenage traumas and felt it best to say nothing. At this point, I was thinking this case was not for the like of us.

Our client looked at us closely.

'Shall I continue?' He asked.

'Please do,' I said. What else could I say?

He continued, 'I have since remarried, to my then secretary as it happens, who was the reason my first wife left me, of course, but my new wife and Megan never got on at all. Megan hated Kylie, my new wife, and the feeling was mutual. Women!' He sighed.

'Jill now lives in New Zealand and we have completely lost touch with her. Megan did not forgive me for my affair and then marrying again. She became cold and withdrawn. I was really out of my depth, and Kylie and I were not really coping with her. She became wild and temperamental, but nevertheless did very well at her private school, where she was, amazingly, a perfect student and never in any trouble. Kids!'

Ian and I nodded sympathetically. I felt ever more a fraud!

'So now she is at uni, in Manchester, you say?' Ian asked.

'Yes, she is and now she does not want to know me at all. She is in her second year and has only been home once so far. I was disgusted by her appearance when she walked though my front door. Plastered with white make-up, wild spiky hair, black lips, panda eyes, pierced rings through her lips, nose, ears, and covered with tattoos, neck, arms, and God knows where else.'

'I threw her out, I'm sorry to say, in a fit of temper, which was really despair, you know?' Mr Wilkinson started sobbing. Pat came in and put her arm around him.

'I still love her,' he wailed. 'I really do.'

I pulled a bottle of whiskey out of my desk but he waved it away. He made an effort and pulled himself together.

'I want you find Megan and report back to me what the situation is. If she needs money, or any other support, I will provide it. If she is happy and not in any trouble, then that is fine. I just want to know that she's OK. Right?'

I made a decision. I felt sorry for the man. I could not let this man down completely. I said, rising to my feet, 'We'll do our very best, Mr Wilkinson. I'm sure your daughter is just going through a mad teenage phase that will soon go away, like so many others when they first leave home and parental guidance.' I was bluffing like mad, of course, but remembered my own time at uni, which helped.

Mr Wilkinson also rose to his feet. His look was steely.

'The utmost discretion is required, Mr McGuire. If my daughter finds out that I've been spying on her, I can't imagine what her reaction might be!'

I said nothing more. We shook hands and Pat showed him out.

When he had left, I described to Pat what he had said about his daughter's appearance when she had come home from uni. She thought for a moment and said, 'It sounds like she has joined the cult group who are called "Goths". It has always been popular at unis not just in this country. I don't know much about them, but I'll research them if you wish?'

'Please do,' I said. 'It may help us to locate her. I don't think it will be a difficult case for us and I felt sorry for the man. It will give us a good experience of basic detective work at its easiest.' Ian looked worried. He was right to be.

Looking back, many weeks later, how wrong can you get!

Chapter Sixteen

Pat had booked us, Ian and I, a couple of rooms in the Manchester Hilton, for the following night and three more to follow. I had persuaded Charles, who was my deputy in all my estate duties, to take over the reins for a week, with me available by phone and zoom if really necessary.

He was better at the job than me, in any case, for obvious reasons. He knew I needed time to get my agency up and running properly. He is a great guy.

We packed our bags and drove in my Range Rover down to Manchester, then booked into the hotel. Neither of us had been to the city before, and I must admit on the journey in, we were not that impressed, being countrymen at heart and all those high-rise buildings crowded along the main roads were ugly in our eyes. We both rather hoped we could get the job done quickly and return to more rural surroundings.

Pat had typed up a report for us to read, about the goths. We learned that it was a cult that started in England in the 1980s based on music like Punk, Death Rock, Bauhaus, The Doors, etc., none of which meant anything to Ian and I.

Basically, she said, it was an anti-establishment movement, popular then and still popular today in universities, not just in the UK, but all over the world. Students tend to want to be rebels, of course they do. It's all part of the growing up process and can be good fun while it lasts.

I remember being at Oxford, we were all rebels too, against authority, whatever it was. Even closet true-blue right-wing Tories like me toyed with Marxism, and such. To impress the girls! And to not appear an old fuddy-duddy, aristocratic bore.

Anyway, as said, goths have continued to be popular and the movement has grown into a huge, world-wide one, in Canada in particular, and Scotland, and even Cuba. It is now mainly a fashion thing. Girls have black, spiky hair, and boy's hair is piled up in peaks way above their heads. Both sexes have tattoos all over, girls have black lips, white faces, and, of course, ripped jeans.

Just everyone wears ripped jeans, not knowing why. Oh, and piercings—rings through noses, ears, lips, nipples even. The basic idea is to look as ugly as possible it appears! They also like horror stories. Their idol, amazingly, is the long-dead American author of such stories, Edgar Allen Poe. I couldn't believe what I was reading, and Ian's face told the same story.

Harmless enough, I suppose, but Pat reported that it could turn very nasty, as girls in particular self-harmed in some cases. They said they hated their bodies and would cut themselves to *punish* their bodies. This could be very difficult to cure and could, and did sometimes, lead to suicide and death. So at least, Ian and I knew what we were dealing with.

It suddenly seemed to be extremely unpleasant. We looked at each other in some dismay, both sitting on my hotel bed, reading the report, with very long faces. What on Earth had we got ourselves into?

Unfortunately for us, our appearance did not lend itself to undercover work amongst students, let alone goths! We looked too old, too like policeman I suppose, being big, tall and muscular, despite us wearing jeans, tee-shirts and trainers. So we needed to come up with a plan or a strategy to try and find this Megan.

Her father had downloaded several photographs of her onto our phones, of course, but the photos were taken long before her goth days. She looked a pale and rather pretty girl, nothing special. Long fair hair and regular features, like so many others. Not easy.

Pat had come up with the best idea we had in our portfolio. She had suggested we try and contact students on a drama course of some kind. Media studies type of thing. We might persuade a student to work for us, for a suitable fee, someone who could act a bit would be ideal in working undercover to find Megan for us.

This would solve the problem hopefully without too much fuss and bother. Students are nearly always broke and looking to make some money, we reasoned. Should be easy enough.

The next day then, after a massive breakfast each, we took a taxi to the university. The taxi driver was very helpful. He was an immigrant from Afghanistan, married with five children all under the age of eight. He knew the university well, including the fact that there were three of them in the city. The main one was the one we wanted, where Megan was a student, based around Oxford Street.

It proved to be an enormous site, of course. Our driver took us up, down and all around enormous buildings. The streets were full of students hurrying along, many on bicycles.

It was impossible to park, as far as I could tell. Oxford Street itself is very long and very busy.

There appeared to be a procession of some kind walking down the middle of the road waving placards and protesting about government immigration policy as far as I could tell. My heart sank. Ian looked at me, glumly. I think that he, like me, felt like giving up the whole case as a bad job.

We instructed the taxi to take us back to our hotel. Meeting that taxi driver was the only good thing that came out of that morning. *He was great and kept us amused with his ceaseless good-humoured chatter, certainly a good advert for immigration*, I thought. Such people are priceless.

Ian and I sat in a lounge area in the hotel and ordered coffee and biscuits. We both thought we would skip lunch to save time. I asked Ian to phone the university and ask whether there was a course dealing with drama as a subject and also ask if we could visit that department with an offer of some acting work for a firm of private investigators.

We thought that telling the truth was probably the best course of action. Meanwhile, I would find a print shop and obtain some printed notices we could, if we managed to get permission, pin up on some notice boards in that department. The wording would be simple—our name and phone number and a brief note asking for volunteers willing to do some acting work for us for a commensurate fee.

Nothing about the job to be done, of course. We would have to be very careful not to appear to want someone to spy on a student! After choosing someone and impressing on that person to not ever reveal to anyone what he was attempting to do, we would tell them what we needed: to obtain confidential information just for the father of one of the students who was desperately worried about his offspring's welfare, after becoming estranged.

The simple truth. We thought this plan would be perfect. At the time.

We were fools. Stupid, irresponsible fools. To be fair, we neither of us were at all happy at what we were doing, but we had accepted the brief and we felt we had to go through with it. We told each other we must learn from this case, and no matter what sob story we heard, we would never do this type of thing again. No way.

So Ian went off to do some phoning, and I went into the city to try and find a print shop. I found a travel information office, picked up a city centre map and asked a very helpful member of staff there for directions to find what I was looking for. The woman suggested I visit the huge Arndale Centre, scene of an IRA bomb outrage many years ago.

She said there was a print shop there, among hundreds of other businesses. I thanked her and started walking. My first visit.

Manchester is not, I suppose, an attractive sort of city. There were no flowers, nor trees, nothing green I could see. Just enormous buildings and fairly narrow streets full of traffic, including metro trams in the middle, honking their horns every few seconds, necessary because the streets were also full of grim-faced people—some riding bicycles, and e-bikes, dangerously weaving in and out. Positively chaotic!

To add to the picture, there were lots of down-and-out vagrant persons lying on the pavements, one on every other lamppost, complete with their dogs, mostly all asleep. Not exactly an attractive city, as said.

I saw two girls, walking arm-in-arm, students, I imagine, coming the opposite way to me. *Two strange-looking girls, with white faces, black lips, spiky hair, piercings in their noses, lips, ears, tattoos on their bare arms*, and I thought, *they must be those goths, that we were told about.* I surreptitiously took a few photographs on my phone, pretending to snap the buildings and the street scenes.

I need not have bothered as the girls took no notice of me. They looked stoned. I wondered if one of the girls was Megan. *That would have been too much of a coincidence surely*, I thought, *but undeterred, I called out, 'Megan!'* The girls continued to walk by of course. Worth a try, I suppose. Nobody took any notice at all, which I thought was odd.

It struck me that in a busy city everyone was anonymous, all intent on doing whatever they were doing, absorbed and invisible. Not a bit like village life, where everyone stops for a chat, pats your dog, no rush, no fuss. I longed to be back in the countryside.

It took a bit of searching, but eventually I found the shopping centre, a vast building on God knows how many floors. I had to ask, at an information desk, directions to a print shop. Incredible place to me. Horrible.

I ordered some posters, A4, full colour, with our logo at the top, and our names, Ben and Ian, just seeking assistance in a missing persons case, with no details, but offering a substantial fee to suitable applicants. A telephone number at the bottom. Simple. The assistant told me to come back in an hour, so I found a café and ordered a burger and a coffee.

I'd bought a paper to read and the hour soon passed. I collected the excellent posters and walked as quickly as I could back to the hotel, arriving at about 1600 hours. Ian was sitting in the lounge area, waiting for me. He did not look happy.

'Hi, Ian,' I said.

He grunted. I find that a useful thing to do myself, a sort of non-committal grunt is very often sufficient a response. I grinned at him and showed him my plastic bag filled with posters. He glanced at them without comment.

'What's up, mate?' I asked.

'Sorry, Ben, just feeling a bit depressed, I suppose.'

'Yeah. I know the feeling. Look, did you do some ringing round at the uni? I mean, let's get this done and get out of here!'

Ian managed a grin of sorts, more a grimace, then said, 'Yes, I did ring around, actually. I've managed to get an appointment with someone from the student union, along with a student from a drama course.'

'Wow! That's great. Well done, Ian,' I said. 'When for?'

'Tonight. Eight pm in the Student Union building. I've booked a taxi. The reason I'm depressed is because this guy we are meeting, who is some official from the union, was not at all encouraging on the phone.'

'What did he say, then?'

'He said spying—that was the word he used—*spying* on a fellow student was very much beyond the pale, but he would have the grace to listen to what we have to say, what we have to offer. I'll be honest with you, Ben, I feel a bit grubby.'

'I know how you feel, Ian, and I feel much the same, but on the other hand, I can feel sympathy with our client. Surely a father has a right to protect his daughter from harm?'

'Well, that's fair enough, in a way, but we must be quite sure that we don't interfere in this young girl's life. We've only heard one side of this story. It's a difficult decision to make and we are totally unqualified to do so, Ben, neither of us has any training, or experience, of such family problems. I'll go along with you tonight, I've got to, but I might very well pull out of this case, unless I feel sure that what we are doing is right for the girl.'

We left it at that and after deciding to meet for dinner in the hotel restaurant at 1800 hrs, we both went up to our respective rooms to shower and freshen up for the interview that evening.

We both enjoyed a huge sirloin steak for our supper, with just one glass of an excellent Malbec wine to cheer us on the way. We dressed down for the interview in jeans and tee-shirts as we thought this would be best.

Chapter Seventeen

We had a long, serious conversation over dinner, discussing the morality of what we were attempting to do. I took the father's side and made the best defence I could think of to justify his concern, especially about the subject of the girl becoming involved in being a goth. We had both spent an hour or so on the Internet researching the cult ourselves, so at least we had tried to understand why kids were drawn to it.

Of course, we agreed it was all tied in with what is called "teenage angst"—the psychological effect of being neither a kid nor a grown-up, battling many sensations coursing through their bodies and minds. Drugs, alcohol, being away from parents, loneliness, feelings of being useless, inadequate, stupid, ugly, or whatever.

Somehow or other, most of us get through it all eventually, thank God, but it is a difficult few years, it really is. It is simply the pangs of growing up, right enough, but that is a facile thing to say.

We did not come to any conclusions, but at least we'd made an effort.

We duly arrived at the rather impressive Student Union building and found the entrance, where we were challenged to show our IDs. We showed him our business cards and explained we had made an appointment with one of the union officials. This seemed to satisfy the guy and he then led us away to a meeting room away from the main drag. He then went off and found the guys who had been expecting us and introduced us to them. Grant and Glen, first names only.

They were dressed like us in tee-shirts, jeans, and trainers. I showed them my posters and explained that we basically wanted to hire an actor, male or female, to find a student, from among the 12,000 strong student body, simply to ascertain that she was OK as she was estranged from her father, who was very worried about her and wanted to help her, should she need it. We explained that the father had hired us, as private investigators, to take on the task for him.

The union official was a solid-looking, heavy set lad, with an aggressive expression on his big-chinned face. He looked like a young Donald Trump. His name was Grant, we had been told.

He said, glaring at me with his pale blue eyes like searchlights, 'Why do you want an actor, then?'

I said, 'Ian and I thought an actor would be able to find the girl without appearing to be a nosy person trying to hassle her. An actor from the student body here could perhaps empathise with her and appear to be just another student being friendly.'

Grant grunted. 'Look, there's no way we can help you unless you can prove, without doubt, that your motives are OK. I can't possibly allow you to spy on this girl and that's that. You will need a fucking good reason, and so far I'm not convinced at all. Why is this girl's father "estranged" anyway? She might have a good reason not to be found by him.'

I lifted my hands in surrender.

111

'Look,' I said, 'I assure you that neither he nor our firm want to know her address or telephone number or anything that might enable him or us to contact her. That is not our client's purpose at all. He respects her right to live her life as she wishes, and he does not want to interfere in her life. He simply needs to know she is safe and well.'

'I empathise that neither he nor us will ever contact the girl and we do not want to know her location, so this will not form a part of any report we make. So if Glen says that Megan is safe and well, that will suffice our needs precisely. Of course, we hope this will be the case, and is more than likely. But if, on the other hand, Glen thinks she is ill or in danger, this will be also be reported.'

'What happens if that is the case? You may ask. At this time, there are no plans to cope with such a problem. This is outside of our brief. It will be up to her father, and we, as private investigators, will *not* be involved this time.'

Grant looked at his companion, Glen, who we later found out was also his best friend. He then asked us if we would excuse them while they had a private discussion. He told us to wait where we were and that they would come back shortly and give us a decision. With that, they left. Glen had said nothing this far.

He was a small and delicate-looking lad, with flowing curly hair, somewhat effeminate, I thought. Pretty, rather than handsome. But I knew such appearances can be deceptive. A colleague of mine and Ian's, in the SBS, had similar build and appearance and he had proved to be the bravest, brightest and best man we had ever served with. As his commander, I had found him to be an amazing guy, totally ruthless and afraid of nothing. A good man to have at your side in battle.

This Glen character had sat through our interview totally relaxed and calm, but the man had what I think actors call "presence"—his deep-set eyes shone with intelligence. While they were gone, Ian and I agreed that of the two, Glen and Grant, Glen was the dominant one and probably the one to make the decisions.

They were gone only a few minutes. The atmosphere had changed, they were both a lot more friendly. Grant once more did the talking. He said, 'We have come to a decision. We cannot give you permission to put your posters up. They might create a security problem. The girl you seek may find out that she is the subject of your investigation, which would be very embarrassing, of course.'

Ian said that we quite understood his concerns and that we would destroy the posters, however Glen asked for a copy, rather to our surprise. We gave him a couple of them which he placed in his folder. He had a really deep, vibrant and resonant voice, which again was a surprise.

Glen then said, 'I will personally take on this task you have set, so there really is no need for your posters, anyway. I will undertake, for a fee to be negotiated, to seek out this girl and find out the information her father requires for you. I must tell you that I will also research your firm and your own credentials. I will obviously need some time to do all this, so I suggest we meet again tomorrow morning at eleven am to discuss terms of reference.'

Grant said, 'Thank you, gentlemen. I will take my leave and leave you and Glen to sort this matter out. I can only hope we are doing the right thing here and I wish you success.'

Ian and I stood up, thanked the two students warmly, and left. We both felt rather shell-shocked by the experience. Ian

113

said, 'Phew, I was really impressed by both those guys, weren't you, Ben. Especially by young Glen. If anyone can do this job, I would say he could. What do you think?'

I had to agree. I said Glen seemed to be totally in control of the situation and appeared to be a most impressive young man. We had dropped in lucky there, we agreed.

By now, it was lunch time, but neither of us felt like eating much. We thought we'd find a pub and have a pint or two and maybe a bag of crisps or something. I fancied a pork pie and chutney, or biscuits and cheese. So we set off walking from the Student Union building, heading in the general direction of our hotel, battling through the milling hordes.

It was not exactly a pleasant walk, but interesting enough, looking at all the massive buildings, from many periods, Victorian splendour to post-modern ugliness. We popped in a fine museum of natural history. It turned out to be so interesting that we forgot about finding a pub and settled for coffee and a bun in the small café there. There were even live reptiles in the museum. A real treasure of a place. Fascinating.

Chapter Eighteen

The rest of that day we just lazed about, wandering the streets. Manchester was working its magic on us, and we found ourselves being drawn into really enjoying the place. I had certainly got a wonderful history that not many cities could emulate, particularly with the Working-Class Movement and the trade union growth, etc. (not quite my thing, of course!) and we were beginning to realise why it is such a great Northern city.

After dinner, we continued walking the streets. Like all big cities, the place was buzzing with life at night. Not really our scene. Two fish rather out of the water. Especially me, to be fair.

The next day, after another monster breakfast binge, thoroughly enjoyed, we set off by taxi for our arranged meeting with Glen.

Glen said, 'I have done some research into your company and was, to be frank, surprised that you are very much new to this game. In fact, to be blunt, you have virtually no experience of detective work at all. Am I correct?'

He looked at us, sharply.

We both raised our hands in surrender.

I said, 'Guilty as charged. After many years in the Royal Navy, Ian and I decided to start a new career as private investigators. We have been joined by a third member of our team as a receptionist and detective combined, and she has had previous employment in a private investigator company.'

'On the other hand, Ian has worked in Naval Intelligence and I have a lot of experience of being in charge of covert operations on her majesty's service, together with Ian, so we are not completely new to investigating and solving problems.'

Glen also made a surrendering gesture. 'Wow! That's quite a CV. Alright, fair enough, I take back what I said.' He smilingly got up and offered his hand, which we both shook warmly.

He continued, 'OK, I'm willing to work for you. I will need some details now, including the name of this girl, of course, and any details you have of her course work this far and anything else you know that could be useful. Grant, as a student union official, does have access to some of the records here, so he should be able to locate her up to a point.'

'It depends on a lot of factors. Our records are by no means complete and are dependent on what the students tell us. We don't check.'

Ian said, 'Before we give you any details, we need to be sure that you will treat this matter with the utmost discretion and not reveal to anyone at all any of these details. You must report only to us. Not to Grant, or anyone else at all.'

Glen nodded his head.

Ian continued, 'I will also ask you for sign an affidavit to that effect, which we have prepared, with legal advice.'

Glen said, 'I'm glad you have said that. I am more than willing to sign your document. I should tell you that at this time, I am taking a master's degree basically in play writing and I already have a LLB law degree, so I think I am a good candidate to work for you on this case.'

In response, Ian dug out the affidavit form from his case and we passed it over for Glen's perusal and signature. He read through it carefully, with a little smile on his face, glanced at Ian once or twice, nodded his head and then printed his name and signed on the dotted lines. I noted his full name was Glenson Thomas Howard, as he passed it back to us.

We then told him what we knew about Megan and passed over a file of information, including some photographs obtained from her father. When I mentioned her father's description of her appearance, the last time he saw her, on the occasion when he had thrown her out of their home, Glen pursed his lips and shook his head sadly.

He said, 'So you think she is or was recently, as far as you know, a member of the goth cult?'

Ian said, 'Yes, Glen, as far as we know, that's the case.'

'And is that the reason, do you think, that she and her father are now estranged?'

I said, 'Look, Glen, we are not really sure of *anything*, but it might have been the last straw for her father. He said that ever since her mother left, and since he has remarried after an affair with his secretary, she has been unhappy and cold towards her father and she hated her step-mother apparently, so it was the culmination of a long period of it being a very strained relationship in the home.'

Ian added, 'But the man was in tears, sobbing in our office, saying that he loved his daughter, over and over. He really regrets the past and wants to make amends. We felt sorry for him and decided to help him.'

'Ah, I see. He would like a reconciliation.'

I said, 'Not necessarily, Glen. As he said, he just wants to know she is safe and happy, nothing else matters.'

Glen sighed. 'I think I understand. As you say, it is complex. Anyway, I'll do as you ask, seek her out and send you report on what I find, as agreed. But we now need to sort out my remuneration. I must confess that money is the chief reason why I have taken on this job for you. I am absolutely skint at present and really need some cash.'

He grinned for the first time, looking quite transformed. I warmed to him.

I said, 'We are offering one thousand pounds, if that is OK with you.'

'That's fine, Ben.'

'I suggest we pay you half now, and the remainder after you have given us a satisfactory report. Do you want cash or a cheque?'

'Cash, please.'

I got out my wallet and paid him five hundred pounds in twenties. He counted it carefully and put it in his jacket pocket. He signed my receipt.

Glen said, 'I'll send you texts every night to keep you up to date with progress, if that's OK with you guys?'

We both nodded our heads in reply. I realised we could have been conned and that we may never hear from Glen again, but that was a chance I had to take. We really had no choice. I just wanted to get the thing over with and out of my hair. It made me feel grubby, but at least we had tried our best. Both Ian and I thought that if this is what the life of a PI is like we don't think much of it.

What we didn't realise at the time was that things would become much more exciting, and tragic, soon enough.

Chapter Nineteen

Ian and I decided to leave Manchester and return back to our Morecombe base. Pat had phoned us and told us she have had another two possible clients contact her and she had asked them both to ring again when we returned from Manchester, but did we want to know? Of course, the big factor for me was that I couldn't let Ian down, or indeed Pat. We really had to make the agency work.

After showing our faces back at the agency, the weekend beckoned and we both wanted to go home, so I told Pat to close down the business a bit early. Ian wanted to take Pat back to his mum's B&B in Wales, for a little holiday, so things were progressing nicely between them. I was back in my new house, where I was expecting Sue to come and visit me.

I had promised to show her around my estate and introduce her to my brother and his family. There were also some documents for me to approve and sign regarding the estate's business interests. I leaned again on Charles for guidance.

Saturday came along, and I went and picked up Sue from John Lennon airport. It was lovely to see her and she was so loving and cuddly. We both were desperate for one and other. We could have spent the whole weekend in bed! The sex really was terrific. I had not experienced anything like it before. Magic!

I'll spare you the details. But apart from the sex, I did manage to escort her around the estate, and the big house, and she was pretty fascinated by my stories about my family history, particularly the bits about my infamous privateer relative, back in the days of Queen Elizabeth I. Sue loved my new rented home and the two staff members looking after me, but I don't think she saw herself living there.

She really loved her home in Ireland and was still full of plans for her new home in Daddy's estate. Problem.

We went to meet Charles and Nancy. Sue and Nancy hit it off big time and Sue really enjoyed playing games with the kids, who instantly loved their new "auntie". It all passed by quickly and it was soon time to take Sue back to the airport and her daddy's jet plane home. We spent some time, while she was with me, discussing plans for some holidays together.

It all looked like we were going to have a golden time together. I feel there should be a "but" at this point! There was no doubt in my mind that Sue was aching for me to "name the day". Mmm. Maybe. Perhaps.

Monday came and I went off to the agency. I would divide my time between estate running and agency running. This was the plan. Mornings in the agency, afternoons back at the estate. It didn't work.

Ian, Pat and I swapped stories of our weekends. I was told that the two new prospective clients had turned out to be both women who were in dispute with their employers after being sacked. Pat had made arrangements for us to meet with them on the following Tuesday, but Ian was not at all keen. He was really trying to pluck up the courage to ask Pat out for a dinner date. It kept him occupied!

I rather thought the girl was more than willing and I told this to Ian, but he really was frightened of being rejected. He has always been shy with women as long as I have known him. I don't think he has ever had a girlfriend in his life, big, handsome guy that he is! I wondered if he was still a virgin. On the other hand, he really did not seem to be interested in any case. Not my problem.

Then it happened. There came a telephone call from Grant, the student union official. Glen had disappeared! Ian tried to ring Glen on the mobile number he had given us, without success. The number was dead, didn't ring.

We had a quick consultation and decided to visit Manchester if Glen did not reappear by the Wednesday coming. I asked Pat to cancel the meeting with the two prospective clients. Both of them then decided to withdraw their cases from us, which was understandable, I suppose. At least, though, we were free.

It was a really worrying development. What on Earth had happened to Glen? The unspoken question was soon answered.

We were all just enjoying a quiet cup of coffee in the main reception area, when the doorbell rang. It was the very first time I had actually heard it. Pat went to answer the door. She ushered in a man and a woman who introduced themselves as DC Bowyer and DS Higginbotham, Manchester police, showing us their ID cards. They both had serious expressions on their faces.

It did not seem like it was going to be a social call. I felt a sudden chill. Manchester police did not auger well.

I invited them to sit down in our clients' chairs and they both did, making our reception area seem small. It was suddenly very quiet. Pat offered them coffee but they both refused.

The detective constable got out his notebook. The sergeant spoke. She was a heavily-built young woman, her hair scraped back, her face round and pink, with thick black eyebrows. Quite attractive really.

She said, 'I'm sorry to barge in like this, but I am tasked with making enquiries about a student from Manchester University, a young man named Glenson Howard. I am notified that a meeting took place between your staff with him on Thursday, the 14 of this month, at the Student Union building in Manchester. Is that correct?'

Ian and I looked at each other. I think we were both expecting bad news would follow. With my heart in my mouth, I answered, 'Yes. That is correct. What is the problem, Detective sergeant?' I was dreading the answer, and the look on Ian's face told me the same was happening to him.

Sergeant Higginbotham answered, 'I am very sorry to have to inform you that Mr Howard's body was recovered from a canal yesterday and there is no doubt that the boy has been murdered.'

Both Ian and I rose to our feet in shock. Pat went white but remained seated.

Ian said, loudly, 'Oh my God!' He also had gone pale.

I added 'Murdered! How? Why?' I know I was not making much sense. We three were all absolutely shattered.

The constable calmly wrote some notes on his pad.

The sergeant said, to Pat, 'Perhaps it *would* be a good idea for you to make us all a hot drink.' Pat nodded dumbly but went off to do the honours.

The constable said, woodenly, in a monotone, 'I know this must be a great shock to you people, but we are here following procedure. We need to interview all of you separately and obtain statements. We will also need to have a full account of all of your movements yesterday, before 10am in the morning, please. You will be asked to provide your fingerprints as well.'

He shrugged, as if to say, "procedures." He was a tall, thin guy, with a straggly beard, and a hooked nose.

The sergeant said, 'After coffee, I am afraid I must ask you to accompany us back to the station in Manchester. We have two cars. We will take you to meet DI Masters, who is heading the investigation into Mr Howard's murder. I expect we will be there some hours, but we will drive you back here at the end of the day.'

We really had no option but to obey their instructions. I did say that Pat was not with us in Manchester, but they insisted she came with them, for some reason that they did not disclose. Being thorough, I suppose.

So, we had to close down the agency, lock the doors, and file out to the waiting cars. A strange experience.

We belted along the motorway and we duly arrived at the police station. It was in a district called Hulme apparently, as this was displayed on the sign above the main door. It was a depressing-looking concrete and glass building, shouting of the 1960s. Ugly.

Chapter Twenty

We were duly ushered into separate interview rooms. It appeared that I, being the owner of the agency, would be interviewed first. So I was sat at a plain table in a tiny room, two chairs either side of the table. A tape recorder or some sort of recording machine one end. A big black glass window, obviously one-way glass.

We've all seen the sort of thing in police dramas on the box. And now I was here in reality. Very strange feeling for me. Not my scene at all. To tell the truth, I was really nervous. Me, a big tough sailor. My stomach rumbled painfully. I was thankful when a female PC brought me in a hot coffee, obviously from a machine.

It tasted horrible, but it was welcome. She even offered a small, plastic wrapped biscuit. Equally horrible, equally welcome.

The minutes ticked by. I don't wear a watch, but it seemed ages. Eventually, a grey-haired smallish man appeared, introduced himself as DI John Mason. He sat down opposite me and switched on the recording device, announcing who was present and the date and time. He then turned to me with a smile. 'Procedures, you know.'

He asked me to confirm my name was Benjamin McGuire. I had to tell him that that was my business name and gave him my full title, showing him my driver's licence as proof. This obviously startled him.

'So let me get this right, Sir. You are the Earl of Sumerton, is that correct?'

'Absolutely.'

'Christ! This is a first.'

'Sorry about that.' I then gave him a quick outline of how I came to be a private investigator, using a false name.

'Christ!' He repeated. Then added, 'So do I have to address you as "My Lord" or something, then, Sir?'

'I think it would be better if you treated me as plain Mr Ben McGuire, as it was in that role that I am a witness here, Inspector,' I said.

The inspector grinned. 'OK, Sir, that's what I'll do.'

He continued, 'Well, Sir, basically I need to ask you a few questions about your relationship with the murdered man, Mr Glenson Howard. Why did you come to meet with him at Manchester University? Just tell me in full, in your own words please.'

So, I told him that I had hired the young man to help find the daughter of a client of mine, who was worried about her, as they had become estranged. I told him that I had paid five hundred pounds to Mr Howard, with a further five hundred pounds at the completion of his report. I said that the last time I had seen him was on the occasion when I gave him the cash deposit and I confirmed the date and the time this had taken place.

The inspector said, 'And that was the last time you had contact with the young man? No phone calls, no contact at all?'

'That's correct. Although, I must confess that I have not checked my mobile phone for a day or two. I have it switched off most of the time. I realise that this is foolish, but I am very new to this game; it is my very first real case as a private investigator, after many years' service in the Royal Navy.'

The inspector rolled his eyes at this, then responded, 'I must ask you for your phone, Sir, procedures, you know. It will be returned in due course.'

I was not happy about this, but I had no choice, so I handed it over and told him the password.

I queried, 'Am I a suspect, then, Inspector?'

'Oh no, Sir, simply a person of interest.'

He continued, 'Now I must ask you to tell me the name of your client, and the name of his daughter, the girl you asked Mr Howard to find for you.'

Again, I had no choice. It was a murder enquiry and I wanted to give the police every assistance I could.

I said, 'I will need to contact my client and inform him what has happened, of course. We were at the very start of this case and to tell the truth, we were hoping that Glen, Mr Howard, that is, would be able to find the girl easily enough and tell us what the situation was with her. My client has no wish to do anything other than reassure himself that she is doing alright at the university and is safe and well.'

'You see, the father has totally lost contact with his daughter. She has rebelled against her father and wants to be entirely free of parental control. My client accepts this totally, but just wants to help her, should she need it. He is worried that she has joined a sub-cult sect of some sort.'

'I see, Sir. Now which sub-cult sect are talking about?'

'I believe they are called Goths, Inspector.'

'Ah. Well, of course we know about this cult, Sir, it is just a fashionable thing that appeals to some youngsters. We generally have no trouble from them. They are pretty harmless, on the whole, like punks and other exotics as the call themselves. It is just a phase some youngsters go through. However, in this case, we will have to look into it, of course. It could be a factor, if some of the group thought that Mr Howard was spying on one of their number?'

He looked at me quizzically.

I said, 'Our researches have shown goths to have a love of violence, horror, that sort of thing. Their bible is the works of the American Horror writer, Edgar Allen Poe, so-called "gothic horror".'

'Really, Sir. Well, as I say, we will look into it.'

The inspector switched off the recorder, after saying the necessary closing words, then rose to his feet, saying, 'I think that will be all for now, Sir. The facts of this interview will be typed up for you to sign before you go, Sir. I should say that your colleagues are being interviewed by my officers as we speak.'

'I must ask you to wait here, Sir, for fingerprinting to take place as the next step. Thank you for your co-operation, Sir. I will get some refreshments sent in, sandwiches and a hot drink.'

'Do I get a choice?'

'Not really, Sir. Cheese and ham are likely, I am afraid.'

'Fine.'

The day ground to a close. It seemed to take an eternity, but eventually we were driven back to our office. Our phones returned. We were exhausted. Who suggested being glamorous PIs then?

I tried my best to get some information from the inspector about the murder, but he was not helpful. 'Better leave the murder investigation to the professionals now, Sir, we don't want amateurs messing things up for us. No, leave it to us, Sir, and that's not a request.'

But I thought that I must find out for myself who it was who killed Glen. I felt it was my responsibility, my fault. Glen was a superb young man with a great future ahead of him and I had taken that all away. I felt guilty.

We filed out of the station and into the waiting car. We did not speak to each other at all. Our gloomy faces told a story.

On the way back, I looked at my phone, in the police car. To my horror, I saw a long text message for me. From Glen.

Shit!

Chapter Twenty-One

I was sitting in the front seat, alongside the driver on the journey home. On the motorway, the young black police specialist driver had switched on the sirens and flashing lights and had belted along at 130 mph. He grinned at me and said, 'Need to practice, Sir.' It was very exciting, I must admit.

I turned to face Pat and Ian in the back seat and saw that they were enjoying the experience, too. I didn't find that text message though until we had turned off the motorway and were proceeding at a normal speed. I had involuntarily yelped "Shit" out loud, and obviously Ian, Pat and the driver all looked at me in astonishment.

I turned and gave my phone to Ian. 'There's been a text message from Glen, Ian! I'm devastated. I'm such a fool. Will you read it, mate. I'm so sorry.'

'What! Oh, Ben, Ben. You idiot! Look, let's wait until we're back at the office. I can't read it here. I imagine the police have kept a copy.'

'I suppose so,' I said, miserably. All those years in the navy, I had never bothered with a mobile phone. It really had been no use to me. Sort of an excuse, but now it was unforgivable. Glen had said he would be sending me daily reports on progress and I had completely forgotten about it. Shit! Shit! Shit!

We filed back into the agency office, and I switched on the coffee machine. None of us wanted to go home. Not yet.

We sat and drank our coffee and tried to gather our thoughts together. Ian have had more success than me in gathering information about the murder. He had chatted up one of the secretaries and she had taken pity on him.

He was a very attractive man, of course, but I was surprised at him—he must be coming out of his shell with women now he has worked with Pat! Using an old-fashioned term I suppose, he might be said to be *courting* our colleague, in his bumbling way. Good for him! I blessed the fact that he was with me.

Ian said that the young lady had told him that Glen's body had been found in the local canal and it had shown signs of him having been tortured. She had obviously enjoyed telling him the gory details, but she did not know, or would not tell him much else. At least, it was something. We now knew it was a really nasty murder and that Glen had died in a horrible way. It made us all the more determined to bring the perpetrators to justice.

I said, 'OK, Ian, you've done well. I've just been worse than useless. Come on, put me out of my misery. Read out the text on my phone, the one from poor Glen. Honestly, I feel such a stupid fool.'

'Yes, that's about right,' said Ian. But he was grinning at my discomfiture. He continued, 'Right the text—actually there are two texts. The first one, from the day we left Manchester, after giving him the deposit money, goes, *Hi, Ben, this is the first report, dated 14 June. I had no trouble locating Megan Wilkinson and I must thank Grant for that.'*

'As a student union official, he has a full database of all 12,000 students here at this uni. As he said, though, this information is supplied by the students themselves and is not checked, so treat it with caution. Anyway, he told me that Megan is a second year student studying Politics and Economics.'

'She has not updated on where she is living though after her first year where she was in student accommodation in Oxford Street, along with hundreds of other first year bods. I will wander over there later and see if I can find out where she is now. I doubt if she is still in student accommodation, though. Virtually, all second-year students move into private rented flats and houses, with their friends. It might be difficult locating exactly where she is living. End of first text, Ben, Pat.'

'I'll read out the second one, which is a lot longer: Hi, Ben, where are you? Anyway, here's my second day's report. I managed to find a girl who knew Megan in the first year. She rolled her eyes at me but told me that she could be found at a pub called "The Slug and Lettuce", known by the kids as "The Slug". Apparently, this is where a lot of Goths meet up. So, I went there.'

'Well, Ben, Megan was there all right and she is a sight to behold. I haven't met her or talked with her, just observed her from a distance. She was wearing torn black jeans, big mass of spiky black hair, white face, black lips, red eye shadow, many piercings, nose cheeks, ears, lips, you name it. She seemed to be some sort of leader, surrounded by her *mates, of both sexes. One of the men was massive and seems to be her bodyguard.'*

'Standing at the bar, I asked a guy if he knew who she was. He told me her name was Souxie (he spelled it for me) pronounced Suzie. The gang surrounding her were her "Banshees". He warned me to keep well away from her. He described her as "evil". He looked scared and bolted after telling me that, leaving his drink behind.'

'Megan, or Souxie, turned and looked directly at me. I must confess she is a frightening creature. The look she gave me was weird. One thing that is certain is that she does not want help from her dad. She is obviously in her element. I strongly suspect she has dropped out of uni and is living in a squat somewhere, unknown.'

'Frankly, I don't want to carry on with this, Ben. Sorry, mate, but I have got cold feet. I await your response. Glen.'

I said, 'Shit!'

Pat said, 'I've heard of a band called "Souxie and The Banshees", I think, but they were well before my time. It looks like Megan is simply resurrecting the name to suit her purpose. I'll look them up on the Internet. Some sort of punk band, back in the 1960s or 70s, I think. It seems fairly obvious who is responsible for Glen's murder, doesn't it?'

Ian said, 'I only hope Glen did not try to contact that girl that night. If you had replied, I imagine you would have told him to abandon his task for us, as being too dangerous.'

I nearly said "shit" again, but instead just hung my head, feeling more than ever responsible for Glen's death. I muttered, 'Of course, I would have told him to stop; God!'

Pat said, 'Look, it's no use blaming yourself, Ben. We just don't know. I think maybe the harm had already been done. Glen said the girl looked directly at him. I think she knew he was asking about her. She wouldn't have taken kindly to being spied upon. I think that you replying and telling him to stop might well have been too late. It sounded to me like he was waiting for your reply before taking any further action.'

'God! I hope you're right, Pat. Thanks, love,' I murmured, not looking at her, still staring at the carpet. *What a lovely, kind, caring girl she is*, I thought.

Ian looked thoughtful. He said, 'Thinking about it logically, I feel I must share any blame here, Ben. I know about you and tech stuff. You are really and truly a technophobe, no idea about computers or smart phones and such. I should not have trusted you to be the one Glen communicated with, or at least I should have asked you about receiving any reports.'

'It's just as much my fault that we have made such a hash of things. I'm sorry I have been hard on you, mate.'

I said, 'OK, fine, thanks, but I can't accept that. Look, lets draw a line under what has happened and concentrate on where we go now.'

Ian added, 'Right, but the other thing that occurs to me is that we neither of us had any idea that Glen might be murdered, or that what we were asking him to do could be dangerous for him. We must, in future, be much more thorough in thinking these cases through, and looking for anything that might go wrong.'

'We must take a more serious attitude to the job, not treat it as a hobby for ex-navy bods looking for a bit of excitement in our lives.'

Pat said, 'Anyway, how do we know Glen's murder had anything to do with his investigations about Megan, who sounds a horrible little creature to me. We really know nothing of any other problems the lad might have had. Gambling debts, Drug gangs, whatever.'

I looked at Ian. He looked at me. Stunned, the pair of us.

We left it at that. It was late and we had had a long, tiring day. Pat went back to her studio flat, Ian and I back to my house (Ian stayed with me during the week now and went back to Wales to his mum at the weekends).

Chapter Twenty-Two

The next morning, we had another meeting to discuss the way ahead. It was a beautiful morning and the scene outside our windows of Morecambe Bay looked tempting. We could be outside enjoying ourselves. However, we were where we were. To my shame, the thought of solving a murder was also tempting. I'm only human.

I had slept badly. Ian and I had had several large brandies before going to bed, but it hadn't helped me sleep. I told myself that I was the leader of the agency and I must devise some sort of a plan. This went round and round in my brain all night. But at least I had made a start. I got up at five am and wrote some notes for the meeting.

After morning coffee and some desultory chat, I called the meeting to order.

I said, 'I have been working on an analysis of the situation we have found ourselves in. I have written down some ideas, so we will start off by discussing these, folks. We have several options open to us, as I see it.'

'One, we could leave it to the police. They have told us to do this, but they have no power to stop a private investigation, so we can ignore that. As private investigators, we can do things the police can't do. But they have the knowledge, the means and the staff numbers to investigate far more thoroughly. Anyway, I think we must investigate for Glen's sake and for his friends, and his family's sake.'

'So, even if what Pat here said last night is true about his murder might have nothing to do with his investigation of Megan for us, we will definitely go ahead ourselves I think?' Ian and Pat nodded their heads.

I continued, smiling gratefully, 'Two then, we must contact our client, Mr Wilkinson, hopefully before the police do. They will certainly want to interview him I am sure. We need to keep him informed of any decision we make now.'

'Three, contact Grant, from the student union. Another guy we need to keep in the loop. He said Glen was his best friend. I think we should ask him to help us in our investigation, as well as in the police investigation. This could be very useful to us.'

More vigorous head nodding from Ian and Pat. They were sitting very close to each other, I noted. I smiled again.

'Four then, we start our own investigation. I think we should start by Ian and me going to that pub, The Slug and Lettuce pub. I think Ian and I should just get ourselves a pint and sit there observing what's going on. I reckon our presence is going to cause a stir among the crowd in there.'

'We will look like police detectives of course and we, perhaps, should encourage that idea. My idea is that if we stir things up a bit, there will be a reaction of some kind. I hope so, anyway. What do you two think?'

Pat said, 'What about me?'

Ian said, 'No, Pat, it is too dangerous. Ben and I are used to this kind of thing and trained to react to any situation that presents itself. We already feel guilty about involving Glen in our plans, I could not cope with you in danger, no way!' He looked really agitated.

I nodded. I said, 'I have a service revolver and ammo. We both will carry knives. This is no job for you, Pat.'

She did not look at all happy but seemed to accept what we said.

She then said, 'Alright, I'll look after the office for now, but remember that I am one of the detectives here, not just the office manager. While you are away, I might take on any cases that come in all by myself! But I have an idea. If you go to that pub, why don't you put up a notice somewhere on one of the walls, or if there is a notice board, asking for information about the murder. That will certainly cause a reaction I would imagine.'

I looked at Ian. Ian looked at me. We both laughed. I said, 'A great idea that, Pat, you can just come up with ideas like that and act as the brains of this outfit, because you seem much better at that job than we are. We'll do the dangerous stuff, you supply the ideas. That's the answer.'

We decided it was time for more coffee, and biscuits. My head was spinning wildly. That brain injury of mine was probably the reason. That was why I had to retire from the Navy. Worrying really. I needed a good night's sleep. I hoped I was up to the job. Time will tell. I had some pills to take if things got bad. I thought I might took them out tonight.

We all went out to a local pub for lunch. I had a good meal and sank a couple of pints and after a while, I felt better.

When we got back, I asked Pat to book us into the Hilton Hotel in Manchester again, starting that night, for three nights. She agreed to do this and added she would contact the police asking for Glen's parents' address, telling them we wished to apologise to them. Surely they would co-operate. She also said that Ian might contact the secretary at the police station again, to see if she could offer any further help.

Ian said, vehemently, 'No way, Pat! I'm not going to get that girl into trouble with her bosses.' He looked thoughtful after, though.

I said, 'Look, folk, we're deep in the mire at the moment. The last thing we want is to sink any deeper. If the police find out that we are nosing around, they could come down on us like the proverbial ton of bricks—on that secretary too!'

Privately, I thought that should the opportunity arise, I might not be as thoughtful as Ian and Pat. I can be ruthless when I think it necessary. All that to come later.

Chapter Twenty-Three

On the principle of "know thine enemy", both Ian and I, and Pat, continued our researches into goth culture. For instance, I had looked at the history of the movement, starting with the Visigoth fanatical hordes, who, apart from fighting other goths, fought the Roman Legions to a standstill at the time of the Roman Empire.

Then followed the architectural revolution when buildings became very different from classical forms, developing sharply-defined pointed arches and windows, which scholars of the day called "Gothic", meaning "ugly" at that time, but not today, of course. Gothic Cathedrals are much admired, for example.

In modern times, anything dealing with death, murder, warfare, space, the supernatural, monsters, vampires, zombies and suchlike may be lumped under the term "Gothic Horror". The kids dressing up as Goths today probably have little or no idea of this history; and whether any of this would help us in our investigation or not, was unclear, but I thought it was necessary.

Anyway, we piled into one of our Range Rover fleet cars, Ian and I, and set off back to the Hilton Hotel in Manchester, feeling we had done our homework. We grabbed a quick meal before setting off in search of the Slug and Lettuce pub, dressed in navy blue jeans, white tee-shirts, trainers, and black leather jackets, with the collars turned up.

We had practiced swaggering and pretending to be police detectives, as seen on TV, like Starsky and Hutch, and practised a sneering expression in the mirror. It really was quite fun, much more like the sort of life we wanted as PI's. We were young men, after all, with a thirst for adventure in our genes. This was great.

It was easy enough finding the pub and we arrived there quite early in the evening, by taxi. It was packed with unsavoury-looking people, mostly young, but some really old specimens among them. Nothing in between. They all looked daggers at us as we entered, swaggering, as practiced. It had gone really quiet.

We ordered pints of lager and stood at the bar, looking moodily around at the crowd. There were a few goths, but I did not see anybody who looked like she could be our target for tonight, which was disappointing. However, we didn't have to wait long for some reaction to our presence.

A large, hairy, aggressive-looking man came up to me and stood very close, invading my space and thrusting his face inches from mine. His breath stank.

He asked, sneering, 'You the filth?'

I stood my ground, despite the stink, and stared back at him, saying nothing.

'You're fucking not welcome in here, fuck off out.' He growled menacingly.

I said, 'Now then, that's not very friendly, mate. We're just enjoying a quiet pint at the bar. What's wrong with that?'

'Bollocks! What do you want? Tell us, then get the fuck out of here, while you can.'

'OK, fair enough,' said Ian. 'We're looking for a girl who calls herself Souxie, we know she comes in here. You know her?'

'What do you want her for, then?'

'We need to eliminate her from our enquiries,' Ian said.

'What sort of enquiries?'

'Murder enquiries.'

'Who got murdered, then?' The guy seemed to have calmed down, he had stepped back away from me a bit. I thought Ian was doing great, really sounded the part.

I said, 'Look, a young man visited here last Sunday night, 15 June. It was the last time anyone saw him, until his body was found in the canal a day later.'

'What's that to do with Souxie?'

'We have reason to believe he was looking for her on that night.'

He came up close to me again, stuck out his chin. 'I'm warning you two, stay away from Souxie, or you will regret it.'

I had a sudden idea. I said, in a very loud voice, 'Look, there is a private funded reward of ten thousand pounds, I repeat, ten thousand pounds, cash, on the table, for anyone giving us information leading to us finding the person or persons responsible for this young man's murder. We are not coppers, we are private investigators. We will make sure there are no come-backs for anyone giving us information. The police are not involved.'

It certainly got their attention. They knew about the murder of the young man of course. I imagine the police had already been to the pub before us. I continued, 'I'll pin my business card by the door. It has our phone number on it and our address. You can reach us either way. We will call in tomorrow night at about the same time, too.'

There was a hubbub of conversations going on as we stood finishing off our pints, which were quite good, incidentally.

A few minutes later, we strolled outside. It was a grim area, litter and dirt everywhere. Even the terraced houses, opening straight onto the road, looked menacing, run down, dirty slums. Not a good place for strangers. We had come by taxi for two reasons.

One was that we did not know the area, the other was that we thought my car might be attacked if we left unattended, a "posh" Range Rover. But now we had to order another Uber.

We stood there waiting after booking one. No-one had followed us out.

Ian said, 'That was a great idea of yours, offering a big reward, it might also have saved our bacon. I reckon we would have had to fight some thugs off by now if it wasn't for that. I could see the greed on their ugly faces.'

'That's true, but I've got my service revolver in my pocket as you know, mate, and we're quite capable of seeing any number of thugs off between us, I reckon. It wouldn't be the first time, right?'

We laughed. It felt good to be back in action, like the old days.

The taxi turned up and we were whisked off without incident. Rather disappointing, that…

But, it was a start, I suppose.

Chapter Twenty-Four

We returned to the Hilton and had a slap-up meal and a bottle or two of wine, so the evening passed by pleasantly enough. Ian and I swapped yarns of our time in the Royal Navy. Happy days. Not bad, then, this life of being PIs.

Ian had rung Pat, ostensibly to give her an update on our visit to the pub. *He is really very much in love with that girl*, I thought, *he just does not want to spend time away from her lovely presence*. I rather thought that Pat was also smitten with my handsome partner in crime! I sensed wedding bells ringing, which would be great. For them.

I was still very much scared of committing myself to a long-term relationship, with having a wife and family. The responsibility of it and the lack of freedom. However, there was no doubt in my mind that wanted to own Sue—I can't put it any other way than the word "own". Exclusive. I was, frankly, worried that while we were apart, she might meet some charmer who would take her away from me.

I hated the thought of this. I worried that I might be a very jealous guy and become miserable, or even violent. Perish the thought. Marriage is not necessarily the solution, I knew. Friends of mine had married, started a family and then found it was a big mistake. Divorce can be shattering. It's not easy.

One good thing about Ian's telephone conversation with the fragrant Pat was the news that she had made an appointment for us to go and see Glen's parents. She had been just about to call Ian or me when Ian had rung her. This appointment was to be at 11 am that morning. The couple lived on the outskirts of the town of Bury.

We found it easily enough, taking the Range Rover for a spin. A fascinating journey actually. Bury is a very busy, industrial and historic town, famous for its huge market, more or less attached to Manchester, but to the North, and where Mr and Mrs Howard lived was a sort of leafy suburb within sight of the beautiful Lancashire Pendle Hills, famous for its myths and legends of witches and the supernatural.

It was a large, double-fronted modern house in a nice, tree-lined road, with good-sized, tidy gardens, front and rear.

I rang the bell, and the door was opened immediately by a woman I assumed to be Glen's mother, Mrs Howard. She was a tall, thin, angular lady, with a sharp beak of a nose, pale blue eyes, her blonde hair scraped back. I introduced Ian and myself and said why we had come.

The lady wore rather a lot of make-up and there was a grim set to her thin-lipped mouth. She looked us up and down and then motioned to us to follow her into her house, without speaking. We had put lounge suits and ties on for the visit, of course.

She took us into a rather bare lounge, with uncomfortable-looking leather chairs, plus a huge sort of coffee table in the middle, also bare. There were no family photographs, or any pictures of any kind on display. The only other piece of furniture was a large glass-fronted cabinet containing a collection of silver teaspoons, or at least they looked silver.

An electric fire hung on one wall, with some sort of fake logs effect. It was not switched on. A large radiator under the bay window completed the picture. *A cold and unwelcoming room*, I thought, *probably used for visitors such as us*. It certainly would not encourage anyone to stay long, which was the reason, maybe…

God! I felt so guilty, and I know Ian felt the same. It was horrible being there and having to apologise to this lady. I mentally squared my shoulders to take an onslaught of abuse. Deserved. Fully deserved. God!

There was no sign of Mr Howard, Glen's father. I wondered why.

The lady asked us to take a seat, and she then sat opposite us. For a while, she did not speak.

After what seemed a nightmare pause, she did speak.

She sighed, and then said, 'I assume you are here to tell me what happened to my dear son, Glenson. His father is too upset to speak to you. He is in quite a state, I'm afraid, but I will be interested in what you have to tell me. Please, go ahead.'

She spoke in a quiet, cultured voice, like a doctor facing a patient. She did not appear angry or upset, just "interested" in a calm sort of way. I was impressed. I couldn't imagine how I would have felt if it had been my son that had been murdered, but I didn't think I would have been able to speak like this lady had just done. No way.

I said, 'First of all, Mrs Howard, my colleague, Ian, and myself would like to offer our sincere condolences on your loss.'

The lady inclined her head, regally, but said nothing.

I continued, 'Ian and I are partners in a newly set-up firm of private investigators. Our very first case, the one where your son was involved, was to find the daughter of our client. She is a student at Manchester University who is estranged from her father because of family problems. The father just wanted to know that his daughter was well and happy.'

'He did not want to interfere with her life except to offer help if she was in trouble. We decided to hire one of the drama students to find this girl for us, as we thought, perhaps foolishly, it would be easier for someone of her own age, a fellow student, to find her and to report on her to us.'

'The student union offered help in finding a volunteer for this task, after being confident that the girl's privacy would not be usurped and that the girl's whereabouts would not be revealed to the father, just the answer to his question as to whether she was well and happy, which seemed a reasonable request.'

Mrs Howard said, 'I see. The police have not told me any of this. My husband and I had no idea that Glenson had taken on this task for you. I imagine you were offering payment?'

'Yes, one thousand pounds.'

'I see.'

Ian said, 'Look, Mrs Howard, at the moment we have no idea who murdered your son. We think that whoever did this may have been under the impression that he was spying on the girl, but actually his death may not have had anything to do with the girl at all. We know nothing of the background of your son's life at uni, but we do feel guilty and responsible that we may be the cause of his death, so we are going to continue to investigate the crime.'

'The police, as you know, have arrested a group of goths and we know that the girl in question was a member of that cult. This was one of the reasons why the father was worried about her safety.'

I added, 'Please accept our deepest apologies. We are both absolutely devastated at what has happened. We only met your son briefly, but we were really impressed by what a fine young man he was. We are so sorry.'

'Thank you. That means a lot. As you say, there may be many reasons for my son's murder, it is not necessarily your involvement to blame here. But I do thank you for coming here and explaining what has happened. I will tell my husband what you have said when he is calmer. Please leave now. I have your number if we want to speak to you again.'

She got to her feet and walked quickly out of the room. We followed behind her as she opened the front door for us. We walked out and she closed the door firmly behind us. I could hear her sobbing. I guess she had just managed to hold her emotions in check until we left.

How awful for the poor couple. I felt dreadful and I know Ian felt the same. God!

Chapter Twenty-Five

The rest of that day was without incident. We had a pub lunch, pie and chips, couple of pints of real ale. We wandered around until dinner time, at the hotel, had a meal, couple of glass of wine. We hardly spoke to each other at all. The weather didn't help. It had become wet and windy, very familiar in the North West of England, unfortunately, whatever the season.

Ian had been looking at a few newspapers at the hotel. He suddenly showed a lively interest in whatever he was reading.

He called out to me, 'Hey, Ben. There's a piece about Glen's murder!'

He said, 'It's quite a big story, about Glen's biography, and it has some useful details of the police investigation, mate.'

He passed the paper over to me. It was a local newspaper.

I said, 'Good idea, Ian, what *would* I do without you.'

He grinned with delight.

The article read:

Further to the dreadful murder of Manchester University top student, Glenson Howard, our sources have learned that the police have arrested five suspects, all of the Goth persuasion.

There followed a section briefly describing the goth subculture, which I skimmed through. Nothing fresh as far as I could see.

The article continued with a concise biography of Glen himself, describing him as a brilliant scholar, already with a first-class honours degree in Law, and now engaged his master's degree in the performing arts, which had been an absorbing pastime for the young man from his early years.

The article detailed that he had been a member of an amateur dramatic group in his area and had taken on major roles, including the lead role in Hamlet, a performance critics had described with much praise.

The writer then gave some background information about Glen, his parents, and his disabled brother. He described Glen as a much loved and respected youngster and that it was a tragic loss of a fine life.

There followed:

The police have issued a statement about their progress in the murder investigation, which reads, "The brutal murder of this fine young man has shocked the community. We are determined to bring the perpetrator or perpetrators of this dreadful crime to justice. As part of our investigation, we have arrested five members of a local goth group who are currently being questioned.

Mr Howard's dead body was found floating in the Leeds and Liverpool Canal. He had been subjected to the most heinous torture before being dumped there. The police are anxious that any member of the public who has any information, however trivial it may appear, to make this known to the police without delay. The last known movements of the victim are yet to be determined."

The report ended with a secure telephone number that members of the public should use to contact the police about the case. It also stated that the newspaper was offering a five thousand pound reward for information leading to bringing the perpetrators to justice.

I said, 'Wow! That's fifteen thousand pound reward on offer now, together with my offer. That should have some effect, I reckon. That's a useful article. Well done, mate.'

Ian said, 'The fact that the police have been harassing the goths group explains the reception we got at the pub last night, Ben. It also explains why there was no sign of Megan or her gang. I wonder if the police have got any evidence, or are they, like us, clutching at straws, hoping for a break.'

'They must have found out, from Grant perhaps, that Glen was looking for young Megan. We must contact Mr Wilkinson and put him in the loop, Ben.'

'Indeed, Ian. Ask Pat to make an appointment, will you?'

'Wilco.' He grinned. I grinned at his wit. Wilco is a contraction of the phrase "Will Co-operate", and is used as a shorthand message in the armed forces, but as the man's name is Wilkinson…clever sod!

I said, 'Actually, the police probably do not know about us going to the pub and offering a reward. I reckon that if they find out, they'll come down on us like a ton of bricks.'

'Surely they will be grateful for the reward. That should bring in some response, I would have thought.'

'Perhaps you're right. We'll have to wait and see what happens. I wasn't thinking of working with the police and I know that would be anathema for them anyway. If we get some information, I wasn't intending sharing it with them, Ian.'

'Not unless it was absolutely necessary. I mean if we do find out who was responsible for the murder, surely we will have to involve the police?'

'Maybe, Ian. We mustn't take the law into our own hands. It's not like when we were fighting terrorists in Iraq, where we could kill the bastards, unfortunately. But I may be tempted, nevertheless. Why should the swine who tortured Glen and dumped him in the dirty water of the canal live in some comfort living off the state, in prison, when Glen is dead, mate? Where's the justice in that, then?'

'Sorry, Ben. Just can't go along with that, I'm afraid.'

'Fair enough, mate. We'll leave it there for now.'

But secretly, I had my own agenda.

The time came for us to return to the Slug and Lettuce pub, at the end of those miserable slum-like terraced houses. I now knew they were rented out to students as multi-occupied room lets. The squaller was unimaginable but they were cheap. A jolly Pakistani gentleman owned the lot. The tenants loved him.

Again, we used a taxi to take us there. Again, we stood at the bar and ordered a pint of beer each. This time, however, there was a lot less attention paid to us, we made virtually no impact at all. I noticed that the business card I had pinned up had gone. Ian and I sipped our pints and waited to see what happened.

Ten minutes went past, then twenty, then half-an-hour. Nothing. We were still ignored. We ordered another pint each. The guy who approached us last time was not present, nor were there any Goths to speak of. I wondered if the police had made any progress interviewing the ones they had arrested. *The atmosphere was still menacing* I thought, *or was I imagining it?*

I was, frankly, getting bored. I whispered to Ian, 'I don't think this is getting us anywhere. Let's go and have a walk around outside.'

So we drained out pints and left the pub. Nobody, as far as I could see, looked up as we left. Odd, that.

We started walking along past the terraced houses. Every four of them had an alleyway between it and the next block. I noticed a young man sneaking a look at us and then dodging back into one of these alleyways. I nudged Ian and he nodded his head to inform me that he also had seen the movement.

As expected, as we passed by the alley, we heard a loud "psst" sound. We stopped and listened. There were some wheely bins up against the wall and a figure emerged from behind them and beckoned to us to follow him. So we did. He moved fast. So did we. The alleyway was full of debris and stank to high heaven.

Ian grinned at me. He was enjoying this. So was I. At last, an adventure to set the pulses racing a bit.

After emerging from the other end of the alley, the shadowy figure up ahead turned right along a road which appeared be flanked by the backs of some commercial properties. In about 50 or so yards, the guy went through a gateway on the left. It led into a small courtyard, smelling strongly of curry.

There were large pipes and venting on the walls and a small door. The young man opened the door and went in. We followed.

It was brightly lit, a sort of passageway. The guy turned out to be Asian in appearance, small and wiry, with bright intelligent eyes in a brown, bearded face. He looked fierce, but he flashed us a sparkling white set of teeth in a wide grin. We grinned back.

He said, in an unexpected strong Manchester accent, 'I can tell you who murdered your friend, but first let me introduce my brothers. This is a restaurant. My brothers are chefs here.'

He knocked on a door. It opened and two more Asian guys came out into the passageway wearing chef costumes. They also were grinning widely, but both were carrying vicious-looking knives. The message was clear. If we stepped out-of-line, we would be killed. Fair enough, no quarter given, none asked. I was impressed, to tell the truth.

We nodded at the gentlemen in question and they nodded in return, then withdrew, closing the door behind them.

There was another door opposite, and the young man opened that and led us into what was obviously a storeroom, stacked with crates and boxes of all kinds. The smell of curry was strong in here. Rather overpowering. There was also a small table and two benches. We sat down opposite each other. I had a powerful desire to sneeze but managed to avoid it.

I said, 'OK, we get the message. Fair enough. I suppose you want the reward I offered?'

'Got it in one, mate.'

He added, 'So what are your terms?' He was no longer grinning. He really did look fierce. I took to the lad, he was good.

Ian and I had had a long discussion on what to do should something like this happen, which was pretty much what we were hoping would happen. So I turned to Ian and gestured that he should state our terms. It was obvious that we would have to concoct some story about the reward, some tissue of lies.

No way would I tell him the truth, that I was paying the reward out of my own pocket and that it was merely pocket money to the likes of billionaires like me. We had decided to say that Megan's father was the cash cow involved, without asking him.

So Ian said, 'We are offering this reward on behalf of our client, who is looking for his daughter, the girl you may know as Souxie, but that he knows as Megan. The guy is a rich businessman who just wants to help his daughter, but he is appalled by the murder of the student we hired to find her and so is offering the reward. He feels he is responsible for the boy's death and he wants his murderer to face justice.'

'Simple as that. I must again point out that we have no connection with the police. They have no idea about this offer. Your name will not be revealed, and in any case, we don't know it.'

The lad said, 'I know of Souxie of course, and there is no doubt that Glen Howard was murdered on her say-so. Her gang, the Banshees, as she calls them, kidnapped the kid, tortured and then killed him and dumped his body in the canal.'

'I have heard the gang bragging about it, so I'm fucking sure they done it, OK? I go to their squat, where she and her gang are living. It's an old church hall. They've put screens up and painted the walls and that. I go there delivering take-away meals, like. I hate going there. The girl is a monster. She is evil.'

'I would be delighted if you two can find some way to snuff her out. She is a fucking menace, and she will only get worse. As I say, I know where she and her gang are squatting. The old building; I've drawn a map, it's not far. But they've barricaded themselves in and there are at least a dozen of them.'

'Her partner calls himself "Sid Vicious", would you believe, and she's got a minder, a great big thug of a guy who calls himself "Ron". Thick as pig-shit. They're all as high as kites on drugs and that. The place stinks to high heaven, it needs blowing up, If I were you, I'd blow the whole fucking place to bits. I can get you dynamite if you like. I'll give you the map and tell you where it is when I gets the cash, OK?'

He added, 'Everyone knows about it round here. But everyone, including me, is shit scared of her and her gang. They won't grass her up. I am taking one hell of a risk telling you this, but I don't think Souxie and her gang would take on us Pakistanis. If they start on us, they will soon regret it. This also applies to you two guys, as well.'

I said, 'OK, OK, we've got the message. Look, you have confirmed our suspicions, which is principally what we want. We will take action against that gang ourselves, now that we are sure she is responsible. One way or another, she will face justice, and so will her gang, be sure of that.'

Ian looked rather startled at that but said nothing. I reckoned I would be taken to task by him later on what I had just promised.

The lad looked us up and down and grinned.

He said, 'I believe you. But what about that reward, then.'

'OK,' I said. 'I imagine you want cash?'

'Correct.'

'I will bring it along tomorrow, and thank you. I'll be here as early in the afternoon as I can.'

'See that you do. I'll be here all day. We have your card.'

Chapter Twenty-Six

The next morning saw us back in our office, waiting for Mr Wilkinson to arrive for his appointment.

While waiting, we brought Pat up to speed, Ian detailing what we had done since the last time we had been together. She had listened quietly to Ian, asked some pertinent questions and expressed her approval of what we had accomplished so far. She then went through what had happened while we were away, at the office, which was not a lot, but she had acquitted herself well by the sound of it.

The agency, largely Pat to be fair, with our advice by phone when required, was really doing a good job on the simple bread-and-butter cases. All this while we drank the first coffee of the day, on arrival, and Ian and I consumed a few delicious biscuits.

Our client arrived on the dot. He walked in briskly, declined the offer of coffee, and when Pat indicated for him to sit, he did so without comment. He was looking very smart, as he was the first time, business suit, silk tie, highly-polished shoes. The very picture of a successful businessman. But his face told another story. He looked grey and anxious, and fiddled about with his hands, drumming his fingers on the wooden arms of the chair.

'Well?' He asked. 'What have you to tell me?'

Ian said, 'We have located your daughter, Sir, but I'm afraid it is not good news. It is quite a long story. Over to you, Ben.'

Mr Wilkinson butted in. 'Is she OK?'

I said, quickly, 'Oh, she is perfectly fine, Sir, as far as we know. Look, I'll tell you the tale, if you will just listen for a few minutes, please.'

'Right. Go ahead.'

'We decided to hire the services of one of the students to help us locate and report on your daughter, Sir. We did this through the good offices of the University student union.'

'Good thinking,' interjected our client.

I continued, 'Yes, we thought so at the time, but it has turned out to be a complete disaster for the student we hired.'

'Oh, why is that?'

'I can hardly say, it sounds so crazy, but the lad has been murdered, Sir.'

'What!' Mr Wilkinson rose from his chair, in alarm.

He spluttered, 'What are you telling me? Is this some sort of a joke?'

'I know how shocking this is, Sir, but please try to stay calm.'

Mr Wilkinson looked thunderstruck. His face grew red and angry.

He shouted, 'Stay calm? Let me get this straight. You're telling me that I am now responsible for the murder of an innocent student. Is that what you are telling me?'

'Of course not, Sir. You are not involved at all. It is entirely our responsibility. Calm down, Sir. Please, just listen, I'll explain.'

Pat said, 'I really think we should all have a coffee.'

Ian and I nodded, and Pat got up and left us to do the honours. Mr Wilkinson slowly sank back onto his chair. He looked shattered.

'But, why? Why has this boy been murdered? Tell me.'

'It appears that the perpetrators thought he was spying on them. You'll have to be patient, Sir, I will explain, but it is complicated.'

'Oh, right, right. I'm sorry. Carry on then, I won't interrupt again.'

'OK. Well, the main fact we have to tell you, Sir, is that your daughter is safe, happy and well, and doing what she wants to do. It is true that she is a goth, but we are sure this will only be a temporary blip in her life. When she grows up, she will almost certainly be a very different person to what she is now.'

'You see, Mr Wilkinson, we did have a report by text from the boy we hired on the night before his murder. He stated that he had traced your daughter without much trouble and, as I have just said, he stated that she was enjoying her life in Manchester, living with a group of friends and appears to be actually the leader of the group, in that she appears to be the one who calls all the shots, so to speak.'

'So you see, Sir, as far as my firm is concerned, your case is closed, as the deal was that if she was deemed safe and well that was all you wanted to know and that you did not want to interfere with her freedom to live her life as she wanted so to do.'

Of course, what I had just said was a pack of lies, which Ian, Pat and I had decided upon earlier. We decided between us that we did not want to involve Mr Wilkinson any more in our investigation of Glen's murder. We did not have the heart to tell him that his daughter was an evil bastard who had ordered the torture and the murder of the poor lad.

We only told him of the murder at all on the assumption that probably the police would want to interview him at some point, as the person who had hired us. Indeed, we were surprised that he had not already been interviewed as such.

Mr Wilkinson looked relieved. He looked different immediately. Proud.

'Ah, that is good news indeed. A leader eh? Like me. I must say though that I haven't given up hope of one day having a reconciliation with Megan. If you had known her before all this happened—my fault, my fault completely—she really was a golden girl growing up, a beautiful, loving, affectionate daughter. We really were so close...'

He broke off and started to sob. The poor man. *If he knew the full story, it would break him into pieces*, we thought. Pat got up and left the room. I know she would have a little cry, probably in the loo. So sad. But it was his fault, true enough, having an affair with his secretary, breaking up his marriage. Common story.

Puts me off marriage yet again. And kids. Too dangerous. I'd definitely rather tackle some armed terrorists in Iraq!

Chapter Twenty-Seven

Ian. Pat and I really did not know what to do next. There didn't seem to be any hurry, and sometimes it's good to step back for a while and think things through thoroughly. 'No use running until you can walk,' as I remember a lecturer at Oxford telling me, an age ago it seemed.

So, as the weekend loomed, I decided to close the office until Monday, all go home, catch up with other matters for a couple of days, then meet again bright and early afterwards, back at the office, with some new ideas for progressing the murder investigation.

Before I went off, of course, I had to go and pay that Asian lad his due. That was simple enough. It closed that episode.

So, I went to Ireland to spend the couple of days with my gorgeous girlfriend, Sue. *Ian went to Wales to be with his lovely mum, and, not unexpectedly* I thought, *he was taking Pat with him!* Things were certainly hotting up in that relationship, which was great. I thought that Pat, and Mavis, Ian's mum, would get on like the proverbial house on fire.

Sue had texted me to say she had some big news for me, and I wondered what that could be. She and I had sometimes been having unprotected sex, so that was certainly a big worry. A baby? Heaven's above!

Sue had sent over the family private jet to pick me up, as usual, from Manchester Airport. In no time at all, I was landing in Dublin. It was early afternoon on the Saturday. I was met by Sue, plus a Labrador puppy! So that was the big news, thank God.

Of course, if Sue had been pregnant, there was no doubt in my mind that I'd really have to marry the girl, of course. Perhaps there was a little bit of regret in my mind that it was just a puppy dog...

The little dog had been given the name of "Roo". Apparently, because he kept bouncing up and down like a Kangaroo, in a frenzy of tail wagging, tongue licking joy. I, of course, grew up with dogs galore on the estate, but I must say, little Roo was a delight. I found out later that Sue loved Winnie the Pooh characters.

Sue had been working on her designs for her Frank Lloyd Wright inspired family house, which she intended to have built on her father's estate in Ireland. She wanted me to look at them with her. She saw the house as being where she and I would live, married or not, when I joined her for weekends, and for longer periods when possible.

This girl obviously was keeping the pressure up on me, but I really didn't mind a bit. I was definitely weakening on the idea of living with her permanently and I realised that marriage was ultimately what she wanted. I mean, we loved each other, that much was certain, so why not?

Brother Charles had done much the same sort of thing, building a house on his father's estate. It made a lot of sense. But did I want to live in Ireland? Again, the question might be asked 'Why not?' I suppose I could run the estate from

Ireland, somehow. Two or three days a week to do my duty, might suffice.

Sue had talked to me for hours about her love of Frank Lloyd Wright's "prairie" style of design in the USA, from the early years of the twentieth century. The houses had broad overhanging roofs, wide balconies, simple geometric shapes in a sweeping horizontal lineage. He had used natural materials, stone and wood, to complement the local landscape.

She had shown me photographs of several examples of Wright's homes and I must admit they were admirable in the extreme. Really beautiful how they blended into the surrounding countryside. Sue was so enthusiastic it was hard to resist.

So, we spent some hours, with her plans spread out on the floor, talking about this house. Not really my thing, but I did my best, and the love-making interludes on the scattered rugs, were fully compensatory. She was the expert of course, a fully qualified architect, and the CEO of her own company, so my job was basically to nod approval a lot.

She wanted me to have my own private "den" and I pretended to be really enthusiastic about this and gave her some ideas of what I would want included in the room. I really don't have any hobbies as such, so this was not easy! I said I might like to build a landscape for my interest in historical sea battles, with a fake sea, model ships, cannons, etc.

I had seen something like this in a TV program. I really probably would enjoy recreating some old sea battles. Military History had been my subject at Oxford all those years ago.

All in all, it was a pleasant couple of days, Sue and I together. We made love a lot, went on walks, met with her four crazy sisters and had a good time being teased unmercifully by them, about us getting married. They were pushing this too and were planning the wedding! Cheeky things.

I know they all wanted to be bridesmaids, of course. They argued a lot about bridesmaids' dresses and things. Just typical, but nice.

Sunday came and off I went back to Manchester Airport, courtesy of the private jet. My mind was in a turmoil of indecision. I wondered what Ian had come up with, perhaps with the help of Pat and Mavis.

At the airport, I was guided quickly out to a waiting taxi and whisked back to my house. There was no sign of Ian. Mr and Mrs Croston knew I was coming home of course, and the house was warm and inviting. Mrs Croston said that she had not heard from Ian. I wondered if anything was wrong, thought about giving him a ring, but decided not to.

He was probably saying a protracted goodbye to young Pat. I was sure he would turn up sooner or later. I accepted the offer of a meal that was waiting for us, and afterwards settled down in front of the TV with a glass of whiskey at my side.

Ian turned up at about 11 pm. He had enjoyed a meal at a restaurant with Pat and had seen her home before coming. He looked well satisfied with his evening, which I was pleased to see. We swapped stories of our weekends.

About midnight, I brought up the dreaded subject of 'What do we do next about Glen's murder?'

Ian grinned. 'You first,' he said.

We had brought the brandy bottle and glasses out. So, I gave him a look, and then poured us both a generous measure. I had a draught.

I said, 'You know me, Ian. Action man. I reckon we go round to the squat where Souxie and co. are hanging out and go in boots first!'

Ian looked horrified. 'No way, Ben. We would achieve nothing and probably end up in jail.'

'At least, I'd have had some satisfaction.'

'True enough, so would I, but there must be a better way.'

'OK. Name it.'

'I agree that we should contact Souxie and her gang, and the best way I could come up with was to go to the squat and knock on the door, making some excuse about our purpose. Perhaps we could say we're from a charity that gives help to the homeless and offer them a cash handout.'

'Once we get inside, if they let us, we can then tell them the truth of the matter and see what the reaction is, further than that I can't offer anything much, Ben. Sorry, mate.'

I said, 'They'll just tell us to, in effect, go away, in no uncertain terms and some interesting foul language as well as to say what we can do with our offer.'

Ian laughed. 'You may well be right, Ben, but the other thing we came up with, that's me, Pat and Mavis, was to find out what progress the police have made. The newspaper said they had made some arrests. Should we try to contact the newspaper reporter who wrote that article?'

'Now that's an idea. Yes, that could be useful, no doubt. Look, should we go and speak to Grant, you know, the student union guy. He was Glen's best friend and he looks to be useful in a scrap, too. He could be a big help and he may have some better ideas than we have come up with so far.'

'The police might be more willing to talk to him rather than to us, as well. We are competition as far as the police are concerned, and a damned nuisance.'

'That's true, Ben. Yes, let's go and see Grant. I'll ask Pat to make an appointment for us. You know, the police have a much better chance of putting these criminals in jail, where they belong, than we have. They can send in specialist teams to look for forensics and stuff, and they have armed squads to raid squats like that. We can't do anything like that.'

'Alright, fair enough, but on the other hand, we can do things the police can't do because they are bound by Human Rights Acts and lawyers and "do-gooders" galore protecting such criminals. That Asian lad said we should just blow the squat to pieces, with them all in it. He was right. Good riddance to bad rubbish. Like we did in Iraq.'

'You don't mean that.'

'Don't I?'

Chapter Twenty-Eight

The Squat

Megan, aka "Souxie", lay on her side, slumped on a stained brown sleeping-bag which rested on top of a filthy camp bed. She was unconscious, as a result of the drug "Spice" which she had smoked incessantly for weeks. The "makings" were in her clenched hand. This was Spice, or Mambo, the dried leaves sprayed with mind-altering chemicals.

The Rizla cigarette papers had dropped onto the floor, which was indescribably filthy. The smell was also indescribable. "Vile" didn't come close. This was her squat.

This was where she and her gang lived perfectly happily. It was their choice, after all.

Brian (in this squat called himself Sid Vicious), her boyfriend, stared down at her. She was wearing a short black dress and it had ridden up exposing her buttocks as she was not in the habit of wearing knickers. He concentrated his gaze on the exposed curves and considered climbing on her back and, as he would put it, "giving her one".

He gently stroked her buttocks until he was fully aroused, but he was frightened to do the deed. If she woke up, her reaction would be violent, and he was a coward at heart. He sighed and moved away from her. He did not live in the squat, he had just looked in to sell his drugs, a regular visit. She sometimes let him shag her as she relied upon him for her drugs supply.

Brian himself did not do drugs. He was a technician in the chemistry department at the university. He was very good at his job; geeky to look at, small and thin with a weak, rat-like face. Brian manufactured spice at the semi-detached house where he lived with his mother; it was the best and the cheapest around, he knew. It made him very popular and made him a lot of cash.

His mother was also an addict. She worshipped her son. She supplied him with the dried plant leaves he needed to spray his chemical mixes, his home-made synthetic cannabinoids, more addictive and much more toxic than cannabis, but with a similar opiate effect—and at a fraction of the cost.

Brian was in charge of ordering chemicals for the university labs and he knew the lecturers did not check his purchases carefully. They could not be bothered, and they found it easier to trust the young man.

At the lab, the young man, neatly dressed in his white coat, crisp white shirt and sober tie, with three pens in his top pocket, was well liked and indeed was very helpful to both staff and students. Many of the students, in fact, found Brian far more helpful than the lecturers, who were often missing and remote. He was particularly helpful to girl students, as might be expected.

The girls ruthlessly used their feminine charms to get him to help them to a good degree. Brian was fully aware of this, and he encouraged it. Of course he did. He sometimes took one of the girls out for an evening, and sometimes they were accommodating sexually. He did rather well, in his own estimation.

He also thought he was a really good lover and could give the girls a really good going over, so to speak, being well-endowed for his size. A happy man. Contented with his lot.

He found Souxie absolutely fascinating and was obsessed by her. She had told him how to knock in a special code at the door to the squat so that one of her gang would let him inside. The door had been reinforced with metal and had several thick bolts. It remained the only door to the old church hall, as the others had been bricked up.

The police had once tried to batter the door down, without success. Neither Souxie, nor any of her gang, had ever been arrested. The goths that were arrested had been at the Lettuce and Slug pub and they had now been released, without charge. An anonymous tip-off had led to the police suspecting goth involvement, but they had no evidence and the investigation had got nowhere so far.

Brian's visit to the squat was coming to an end. He had sold some of his wares to a group of four of the gang who were sitting and playing cards and now he was getting ready to leave.

Another member of the gang was wandering about, high as a kite. He was Souxie's minder. He walked around completely naked. This was Ron. Built like an all-in wrestler. Not a pretty sight, very hairy, very spotty, very sweaty and very smelly. Totally off his head on spice. Brian had to quickly move out of his way several times.

None of the gang were from the university. They were all simply homeless vagrants that Souxie had gathered together. She had been fascinated by Manchester's homeless hordes, had been since the first day she had enrolled. God knows why. She had always been a tough young lady, very determined.

What Megan wanted, she usually got and when she had what she wanted, she would move on. That's what she had always thought. She currently had no thought of moving on, but the day would come, she imagined.

Brian took a last, longing, look at Souxie. He knew she wouldn't wake up for many hours yet. He decided to supply her with a weaker chemical mix in the spice he made for her, in the hope for more sex time with her. All her gang had sex with her from time to time, quite openly, while the others watched, open mouthed with lust, when they were not too high. Brian really enjoyed the experience.

He wandered over to the door, carefully avoiding Sid, but just as he opened it, he saw a tall, well-dressed man standing there, his hand raised as he had been just about to knock.

Brian looked at the visitor, mouth open in surprise.

'Excuse me, young man. My name is Alan Wilkinson. I'm trying to contact my daughter, Megan. I believe she's now using the name of, er, Souxie. Is she available, please?'

Chapter Twenty-Nine

The time had come for our meeting at my agency in Morecombe. Pat had arranged four chairs around the big coffee table in my office, which was the largest room in the suite. Assembled were myself, Ian, Pat, and Grant, who had bombed down from his flat in Manchester on his powerful Triumph motorcycle. He was still wearing his leather trousers, one of the problems of coming on a bike is the "leathers", boots, and crash helmet come with him too.

Pat had found somewhere to store the extras. He was a young, big, handsome guy, no doubt, and he obviously was very taken with the beauty of Pat, too. She looked absolutely gorgeous in her classic business suit, crisp white blouse, and her six-inch heels. Stunning. I fear that if it wasn't for Sue, I would be in competition for that charmer.

But my love of my Sue blotted all such desires firmly out of the question. But it wasn't easy.

Pat handed around coffee and offered biscuits and we settled down with some general comments about the weather and the news of the week. I welcomed Grant and thanked him for coming to join us, at the same time introducing him to Pat making a point that she was also a fully qualified private investigator, not simply a receptionist. Grant said he had enjoyed the ride and loved Morecombe in any case, that it was always a pleasure to be there.

I knew lots of motorcyclists gathered in the town, especially on Sundays. We chatted about this for a short while, until I thought the time had come to do some work.

Ian, Pat and I had drawn up a series of points to discuss, as an agenda. These were:

One: Analysis of the facts we were sure about.

Two: Analysis of speculative ideas, that we were not sure about.

Three: Plan of Action for tackling the problem, which was how to obtain justice for Glen Howard.

Four: Any other business.

Pat had emailed the above to Grant over the weekend and I noted that he had taken out a notebook and pen, from one of his trouser pockets, together with a print-out of the email.

Pat was ready with her trusty MacBook laptop computer, ready to take minutes. I was to act as chairman.

I started by listing the facts as I knew them.

'Fact: Glen Howard had been hired, by our agency, for a fee of one thousand pounds, to find a girl student studying at Manchester University named Megan Wilkinson, on behalf of her father, Alan Wilkinson. Mr Wilkinson told us he wanted simply to determine whether or not she was settled and happy at uni. Also, he wanted to know if she needed any help, whether financial or otherwise, which he undertook to anonymously supply for her.'

'He did not want to contact her personally and did not want to know where she was living, etc. In other words, he did not want to interfere with her life in any way, shape or form, as long as she was settled and happy in her studies. He knew full well that she would respond violently to being spied upon and hoped she would never find out what he was doing.'

'Mr Wilkinson had become very emotional and had burst in tears, telling us how much he loved his daughter and pleading for our help. We, perhaps foolishly, felt sorry for him and decided to take on the case, against our better judgment. We both felt grubby about investigating the youngster, that's Ian and I. But we did not imagine the horror what was to come.'

'Fact: Glen Howard had sent two reports by email to me, detailing each day's progress. The first one was sent on 14 June.'

At this point, I handed out a hard copy of Glen's report, which we all duly read.

Grant said, 'I assume you, Mr McGuire, sent back some acknowledgment to Glen?'

I replied, 'No, Grant, I'm afraid I did not, as I neglected to look at my emails on that evening. I know that this was very wrong of me and I must apologise to you, Grant, as I have done to Ian and Pat already. Oh, and please call me Ben, by the way.'

Grant flushed angrily. He really was a very aggressive-looking young man. He said, 'I can't believe anyone in your position could be so stupid as to not check your emails after sending Glen off on such a dangerous mission!'

I said, mildly, 'You're right, of course. But I had no idea the mission was dangerous at all to locate a fellow student and see if she was well and happy.'

I added, 'And to make it worse, I also did not look at my emails the next day and so missed his second report. Again I can only apologise.'

I got this out of my folder and passed this hard copy around. Grant read it with increasing fury on his face, his veins standing out hard on his neck.

He stood up and loomed over me. 'Not good enough, Ben. Totally crass of you and makes you possibly responsible for my good friend's death! Call yourself a PI, man, you are worse than fucking useless.'

Again, I answered mildly, 'I can understand why you are so angry, Grant, believe me, I feel dreadful about my incredible stupidity. I simply did not give any serious thought to this case, which I imagined as being trivial and which I felt so grubby about that I did not want to think about it. I really am totally devastated by what has happened, but we are where we are.'

'All I can do now is to make amends as best as I can by finding the murderers and bringing them to justice and that's why we are here today. Please sit down, Grant, we really need your help.'

'Fucking Bleeding Hell!' He roared but collapsed back in his chair.

I did not blame him. If it had been Ian that had been killed, I probably would have felt the same as him. Best friends are exactly what they are. They are loved, perhaps more than anyone else in ones' life.

I continued, calmly, 'Fact three is that the police have stated that Glen was tortured, murdered, by multiple injuries, largely by kicking and striking with clubs, then his body was dumped in the Leeds and Liverpool Canal sometime on Sunday or possibly late Saturday night, 15 of June this year. His body was discovered by a woman walking her dog along the canal towpath late on the Sunday, 16 June, following.'

'So those are the facts as far as we know them. I now throw the meeting open to comments and suggestions about the way forward.'

Ian said, 'First, I'd like to defend Ben to some extent. In a long career serving his Queen and his country with honour in the Royal Navy, he rose to the rank of Commander and put his life on the line many times in commando style missions into dangerous places around the world. He was severely injured by a bomb blast in Iraq and had to retire from the Navy and has spent many months recuperating since.'

'Ben is a war hero, but I know for a fact, he was never one for technology, never sent nor received an email in his life before the ones sent by Glen on this occasion. I made a mistake in agreeing with Glen to send his reports by email. He, understandably, sent them to the agency boss, Ben, really the last person to send emails too.'

'They should have been sent to Pat or me. So, I share the blame, but I admit that as a company, we have made a complete hash of things and we are truly sorry. We must learn from our mistakes and see to it that such things never happen again.'

I raised my hands in protest. But Grant was obviously moved by what Ian had just said. He reached across to me and offered his hand to shake. Of course, I shook it warmly. I mouthed a silent "thank you" to Ian. I really felt quite emotional at that point, I must admit.

Pat said, 'I also have a confession to make. Alan Wilkinson rang me while you two were away in Manchester. He pleaded with me to give me a clue where he could find his daughter, he was in tears. I'm afraid I told him about the Slug

175

and Lettuce Pub. I could have bitten off my tongue after I told him, but that's what I did.'

'This was before I found out about Glen's murder, of course. If you want me to resign my position here, I will, of course. I've been ashamed to tell you two, but I realise I must.'

I said, 'Oh my God, Pat. You shouldn't have involved him in this. I hate to think of him blundering about in Manchester. That pub is in an awful district, he'll never get out of there alive if he confronts his daughter there.'

Pat was in tears. 'I know, I know...'

Ian said, 'Now look, alright you shouldn't have told him, but you are a woman, and you have a soft heart. I can understand why you told him. No way will I support your resignation.'

Grant was looking at the ceiling and drumming his fingers on the arm of his chair. What on Earth was he thinking of our firm, now? Shit!

He sighed, then said, 'Alright, alright. There appears to be a lot you haven't told me, Ben. You better fill me in before we go any further.'

So I told him about our visit to the pub in Manchester, and told him the story of the Asian guy and what he had told us about Souxie and her gang, learned while delivering his take-away meals. I told him that we knew where she and her gang were living but had not yet visited the squat.

He said, 'Well, surely that's another fact, Ben. You know Souxie's gang killed Glen, Isn't that a fact?'

I said, 'Not really, Grant. It's not evidence, just hearsay. The police could not act on such information, could they. I personally totally believe that Asian guy is telling the truth that he overheard the gang bragging about the murder, but they may not really have done the deed. They may have been lying just to make them seem impressive. Nevertheless, I am convinced they really were the ones' that killed the poor lad, but that is just an opinion, not a fact.'

I added, 'One of the reasons we have asked you here this morning, Grant, was to ask you, through the student union, to check up on Megan. To find out whether she is still pursuing her studies for example. Basically, to find out all you can about her for us. We think she had dropped out of uni and is living in a squat with a group of homeless men, but if you could confirm this, it would be a great help.'

'Right. I only know the girl as a name on a computer. But I will do as you ask, of course. I will give you all the help I can, in any way I can. If you want to raid that squat, I'm your man, too. I'm pretty handy in a fight.'

For the first time, the lad grinned. It lit up his face. At least, this lifted the gloom at bit, thank God.

Ian said, 'Let's take a break. Come on, Pat, I'll help with the coffee and biscuits.' He looked at her affectionately. She was still dabbing her eyes.

After a short break, I called the meeting to order. *Pat looked a lot happier*, I thought. No way would I ask for her resignation, she was a treasure, despite her admitted error. Everyone deserves a second chance. Especially me.

I opened by saying, 'The news that Alan Wilkinson, Megan's father, knows about the pub is certainly a new and big factor. He is a smart businessman, and he looks fit and tough, despite his age. I reckon he is likely to find out about the squat where his daughter is living and go in feet first, like

I was tempted to do. He may already have done that for all we know.'

'We must take this into consideration. It could be useful, actually, not necessarily a bad thing to happen. I imagine he has taken some of his staff with him, he's no fool, that guy. He would not go in by himself, surely. He may have sorted the whole thing out before we have a chance.'

Ian said, 'Good point, Ben, I was thinking on much the same lines, but do we still need to wait for Grant's researches into Megan? We really have no evidence at all to work with.'

Grant said, 'If I go now, I can report back by tonight, with a bit of luck and a following wind. You and Ian will have to come to Manchester tomorrow and we need to go to that squat and make some sort of a plan about how to gain access to the place. My father is a builder, and in the holidays, I work for him as a roofer. I reckon I could get access through the roof easily enough and let you guys in,' he indicated Ian and me.

I said 'That sounds interesting, Grant. We will discuss this further, but, Pat, will you try to contact Alan by phone? See what's happening his end? Perhaps we should have invited him to this meeting.'

Pat replied, 'Yes, Ben, I'll do it right away. Alan is under tremendous strain. He doesn't know it, but we think his daughter is a murderer. I cannot tell him about what we suspect, so it will make talking to him on the phone very difficult. If we did tell him what we think we know, I suspect he will not believe us, and it is true that Glen's murder could have nothing to do with Megan or her gang. We could be barking up the wrong tree completely.'

Ian said, 'If you had heard what that Asian lad told us, I think you would be convinced he was telling the truth, but of course, he was after the reward of ten thousand pounds, so it could have been a made-up story, no doubt.'

I said, 'No, sorry, I am sure that lad was telling us the truth. If he wasn't, he was a fantastic actor. No, he was telling the truth, definitely.'

There were no further comments, so I called the meeting to an end. Pat went off to ring Alan. Ian found Grant's leathers and helmet and he went off. He did not give us time to discuss his roof entering offer, but we will see him tomorrow, in Manchester.

When Pat returned, she said that Alan was not answering his phone.

Nothing further we could do for now. It was a start, of sorts.

We prepared to go to Manchester again, hopefully for the final time. We did not allow Pat to join us. I hoped for positive action. No more talk. Sort those bastards out once and for all. No quarter.

Chapter Thirty

At the squat, Brian, aka Sid, stepped back as Alan pushed his way inside. He had no choice, Alan was twice his size. He then took off, running towards where he had parked his car. He saw Alan's Rolls Royce parked next to it, with a burly chauffeur, in uniform and peaked cap, just lighting a fag in the driver's seat.

Inside, Alan took in the scene at a glance, and was horrified at what he saw. A huge, totally naked brute of a man wandered about, he moved and looked like a movie zombie. Alan decided he would be no trouble, too off his head to be a problem. Three other men, dressed as Goths, sat at a table which was covered with empty bottles, more bottles littered the disgusting floor.

They were playing cards, after a fashion, and they ignored Alan. They were obviously incapable of much movement, so again no problem. The stench was indescribable. Alan had to stop himself being sick. He gagged and pressed a crisply-ironed handkerchief to his nose.

On a trestle bed in the corner, one of several, a girl lay supine, in a short and very dirty black dress, which left her naked buttocks exposed.

Alan strode over to her and gently shook her shoulder.

'Megan? My God! Megan?'

Tears began streaming down his face.

Megan remained totally unconscious. But she was alive.

Alan could hardly believe what he was seeing. His beautiful daughter transformed into this dirty, smelly, ugly, horrendous creature, with body piercings, tattoos all over, ears, nose, lips, arms, legs—a dreadful mess. But there was no doubt about it. This was his Megan.

Alan's tears turned to anger. He looked at the wrecks of men in the room with hate and murder in his eyes. They totally ignored him, spice has that effect on addicts, they become zombie-like. They were in some fantasy world of their own.

They were certainly not responsible for the state of Megan, of course, just the opposite. But Alan did not know this. He also did not know just how lucky had been his *timing*. The door had been opened, coincidentally, by Brian leaving. Otherwise, he would never have got access. Plus, once the gang had recovered, it would have been impossible to have done what he did so easily.

With one swift movement, Alan picked up his daughter in his arms, turned on his heels and headed for the door. Again, he was ignored. The door was wide open as he had left it, so he emerged into the night and strode over to his car.

Ken, the chauffeur, who knew Megan well of course, from a child, was appalled at the state of the girl, but he helped his boss to load her onto the sumptuous rear seat. Alan held onto the girl in the back, cradling her head in his arms.

He instructed Ken to find a local hospital and quick. Ken started the car, pressed some buttons on the satnav, found what he wanted, and glided swiftly and silently away. He was headed for Manchester's Royal Infirmary, a vast and impressive building in the centre of the city.

In about fifteen minutes, Ken steered the big car into the hospital car park, following the signs to the A&E department. He had to park behind a line of ambulances. Alan jumped out of the car and with Ken's help, he picked up the unconscious girl in his arms and ran into the hospital.

He shouted, 'Someone help me please!'

A male nurse came over and looked at the girl. He nodded, grimly.

'Alright,' he said. 'Follow me.'

He led Alan and his daughter to a cubicle and told them to wait, while he fetched a doctor.

He was lucky. Within only a few minutes, a young man in a white coat and dangling a stethoscope around his neck came into the cubicle.

He had a brief look at the girl, then said, to Alan, 'OK, Sir, what can you tell me about this girl?'

'Her name is Megan Wilkinson and she is my daughter. I found her in this condition in a squat and I decided to bring her here myself as she was unconscious.'

The doctor nodded, then turned back to Megan, making some tests, pulling back her eyelids, examining her eyes with a little torch, taking her pulse and listening to her heart. He turned back to Alan.

'Well, Sir, I'm sorry to say we see an awful lot of youngsters in this condition. An ambulance crew would not have brought her here. She's basically in a drug-induced deep sleep. She has obviously been smoking spice, the zombie drug, by the smell of it. She is not in any danger and will probably wake up in the next hour or two.'

'Quite often they turn violent, you know. There's nothing we can do. If I were you, Sir, I'd sit with her somewhere until she wakes up or take her home and lie her down on a bed or a settee. She will be fine, don't worry. All her vital signs are OK.'

The young doctor looked very tired, his face was grey with fatigue. He turned on his heel and walked out of the cubicle. Very shortly after, the nurse came back. He had clipboard with a form clipped to it. He needed to take some details about the girl. Alan answered as best he could. It didn't take long.

The nurse said, 'Have you any questions, Sir?'

Alan felt numb. He could not think of anything to ask, so he just shook his head.

The nurse, said, 'On a scale of 1 to 10, how satisfied are you with the response we have given?'

'Oh, er, right, thank you, I am very satisfied, so I'll give you a 10.'

The man smiled. 'Thank you, Sir. Now will you take your daughter out of this cubicle please, as we need it for another patient right away. Do you want a wheelchair or help?'

In reply, Alan picked Megan up again and carried her out of the cubicle, just saying a quiet "thank you" as he left.

As he was leaving the building, his phone rang. It was Ian Jones, who had been ringing up every hour trying to get in touch. Alan had ignored several calls while he was trying to find his daughter earlier. This time, he answered it.

'Just hang on a minute, Ian,' he said. He transferred Megan to his chauffeur, Ken, who had been standing outside waiting. Ken went off carrying the girl, making for the car, leaving his boss to answer his phone.

'Yes, Ian,' he said. 'What can I do for you?'

'Hi, Alan, well, we just wanted to know what you have been up to in the last few hours, because Pat told us that she had given you the name of the Slug and Lettuce Pub, and Ben and I wondered what you might be doing to find your daughter.'

'Ah, I wondered if that was what you wanted. First, I must apologise. I did say I did not want to contact Megan. I'm afraid I lied to you and I'm sorry, but we are where we are. Well, Ian, from Pat's information I had no trouble finding the squat where Megan is living. It's a wonder what hundred pounds can buy you in the way of information at that pub.'

'Then I was lucky, some guy was leaving the squat just as I was going to knock on the door, so I pushed past him and into the building. The men inside were all off their heads so were no trouble at all, so I picked up my Megan, who was, and still is, unconscious, and in an incredibly disgusting state. I have just been to the A&E department of a big hospital here.'

'A doctor has seen her and said she is in a drug-induced deep sleep but is OK basically, not in any danger. I'm not sure what to do next, to tell you the truth.'

'Crikey, that's fantastic, Alan. Well done, Sir. I don't blame you for the porky. Look, why don't you bring her to Ben and my house. It's a lot nearer than yours, and you might need some help and support when she wakes up. I'll give you the address, if you like.'

Alan jumped at the offer. He was really worried about what Megan's reaction would be when she wakes up and sees her father. That she had been dragged out of her home, such as it was, by her dad, would not go down too well, he was sure. It could make the estrangement permanent. Alan still had no idea that his daughter was a prime suspect in Glen's murder, of course.

He had considered just taking her back to her squat, sticking her back on her camp bed in the corner and stealing away. He really felt desperate for some help.

Chapter Thirty-One

Grant arrived back at the university. His mind was in a turmoil. Glen had been his best friend for years, since their high school days. However, they had gone their separate ways after leaving school. Grant had always wanted to be a soldier. He had joined up as soon as he was able. He enrolled for three years with a Scottish tank regiment and had thoroughly enjoyed the life, rising to the rank of sergeant.

He had been very tempted to sign on again when the three years had passed, but had kept to his original plan of returning to his studies at university to read a BA (Hons) in Economics and Politics.

He had quickly become involved with the political life of the university and had risen to be an officer of the student union in his second year. He and Glen had continued their friendship throughout and had become very close. At this time, Glen, who had completed a law degree, was engaged in studying for his master's degree in the performing arts.

So they were following very different lines of study at the university, but most nights, they met up and enjoyed a good life together, doing all the things university students do in their leisure time. Neither of them bothered much with girls or girlfriends, in fact they had made a pact to stick together and avoid getting diverted by hanging around with the local females.

Since Glen's death, Grant had found life very difficult. He felt as if he had lost an arm or a leg. Life was turned upside down, so he was keen now to assist Ben and Ian to bring the murderers of his friend to justice. They had wrecked his life too.

He sat down in his shared office and turned on his computer, typed in Megan's name on the student database and then contacted the relevant department of the university asking for the lecturer responsible for Megan's welfare. Every student was given one lecturer as a first contact if they were having any problems, whether financial, wellbeing, social, or whatever.

The secretary of the named tutor answered his call. She rang him back after a short time to tell him that Megan had not attended any classes that term, that her family had been informed, as far as she knew, but was not sure of that. She asked Grant if he could find out what the problem was and let her know. She apologised for not being any more help but said she had been "snowed under with work since the pandemic".

Grant made an angry comment and rang off. He was furious. His reaction, under his breath was to say, 'Fucking typical!'

He then decided to visit Glen's accommodation. They had, for some reason, never shared the same flat, or house. It just had not happened, probably because Grant had been in the Army for the first three years of Glen's courses and Glen was well-established and happy where he lived. Oddly enough though, Grant had never really been inside Glen's flat, which he shared with three female students, from the performing arts courses.

They had always met at his place. Those females were probably the main reason. Grant lived on his own in a flat over a post office in Whalley Range a nice, quiet, area of Greater Manchester.

Before leaving, he rang me and told what he had learned about Megan dropping out of her studies. I, in return, told Grant about what Mr Wilkinson had achieved in removing his daughter from the squat, taking her to an A&E, and now heading towards my place with Megan deeply asleep from smoking spice. I asked Grant to come and join them, when he had finished his investigations.

Grant said, 'Right, fine. I'm just going over to what was Glen's accommodation to interview the three female students he lived with. They might be able to fill in the time Glen spent in his final hours, and some information may be useful. Then I'll come and join you.'

I asked if, while he was there, could he find out whether Glen had spoken of any financial problems. He had told Ben and Ian that he really needed that thousand pound offer and that that was why he had taken on the task of finding Megan in the first place.

'Good idea, Ben. I'll do that, but he hadn't told me of any particular problems, I mean, students are always broke, it goes with the job.'

I told him my address and then rang off.

***

At my home, I sat and waited for Alan and Megan to arrive. Ian and Pat were already with me and we all really just fiddled about. It was difficult to know what to say to each other. The tension in the air was palpable.

I heard the Rolls scrunching on the gravel outside and bounded out. Ken stopped the car and helped Alan out and then they both carried Megan between them into my home. I had given my staff the rest of the day off.

I led them into our main lounge and indicated my chesterfield sofa for the two men to lay the unconscious Megan down. She really did look an incredible mess. Horrible. And smelly. *I would have to have my sofa cleaned afterwards*, I thought. My God! What has the world come to?

Alan had said not a word. Ken went back out to the car for a smoke. They both looked pretty shattered.

Ian put the electric fire on and he and Pat went out to the kitchen to make a hot drink for us all.

I said, 'Look, Alan, I cannot imagine how you are coping with all this, but I need you to give us some information about your daughter. You said, on the phone, that a doctor has pronounced her in no danger, that she is in a drug-induced deep sleep and that she will soon wake up and be fine. Is that the picture?'

Alan was shaking. Obviously now he and Megan were safe, reaction had set in. He stroked Megan's hair, her head was in his lap. He managed to croak, 'Yes, that's about right, Ben. She should wake up eventually. The doctor said that sometimes when they wake up after smoking spice, they turn violent, so I have to warn you about that. I'll hang on to her tight if she does.' His shaking was getting worse.

Pat and Ian had returned with trays of steaming hot drinks and biscuits. Pat took charge of the situation.

She said, 'Calm down, Alan. You're both safe here.'

She set a small table in front of him and place one of the mugs of coffee on it. She added milk and sugar, as she had remembered from when Alan had met us in the agency office. Alan waved away the biscuits but sipped the coffee.

Pat added, 'Megan will be fine. She may be angry and confused, waking up in a strange house, so we will have to cope with that. She will recognise you of course. You need to get a grip on yourself, Alan, and be prepared for whatever happens. Drink your coffee. Do whatever you can to regain control.'

I said, 'Well said, Pat, but I think it might help all of us if Alan tells us how he managed to get Megan away from her gang and leave with her from the flat. I find that astounding, to tell the truth.'

Ian had taken one of the mugs of coffee out to Ken, but he now returned and stood there looking uncertainly at Megan.

He said, 'Pat, could you slip out and buy some nightclothes for Megan and anything you might think she will need?'

Pat smiled approvingly at Ian, nodded her head and headed for the door. There was a big branch of ASDA not far away, which sold such things as well as groceries and was open 24 hours. She was soon back with several bags of purchases. She set them down and came and joined us. She looked at Megan and then all around her, as if searching for something.

She turned to Alan. 'Where's her handbag, have you seen it, Alan?'

Alan, who had more or less stopped shaking, said, 'Yes, Pat, I saw a handbag by her at the squat but I did not bother to pick it up. I'll tell you all what happened. I found the squat, or rather Ken did. I went up to the door and raised my hand to knock but before I could, it opened, and a young man stood there looking at me open-mouthed in surprise. He was small and thin so I just pushed in past him.'

'He ran up the street, I think to his car, though that's a guess. So, I was inside the squat. The smell was appalling, it made me want to be sick, but I walked to the middle of the room, which was vast, a sort of church hall, but a totally squalid mess. There was a huge fat man stark naked patrolling around, but totally off his head by the look of him. He ignored me completely and just kept shuffling around sort of aimlessly.'

'There were some guys, dressed as those Goths I imagine from what I saw of Megan last time she came. These guys were sat around a table. It looked like they had been playing cards. They also were high as kites and ignored me. I saw some trestle camp beds down one side of the room and on one of them lay a girl, half naked, lying on her front. I went over to her saw it was my Megan.'

'I was shocked by her appearance. I carried out, without any opposition. I was just lucky. Well, you can see what she is like, the state she is in.'

'Now I must confess that when I was Megan's age, would you believe, I was a sort of punk rocker myself. I remember what it was like as a student of a university. The squat brought back some memories I had tried to forget. Kids are stupid; we all were to a smaller or larger content, free from parental control and sort of desperate, seeking ever greater things to excite us.'

'I got over it as I grew up and entered the real world, and I hope Megan will do the same. Sorry for this, Ben, Ian, Pat. You are very kind people. Thank you. I won't forget this.'

I said, 'Thanks, Alan, that means a lot.'

At this point, the doorbell rang. It was Grant. He strode in taking off his helmet and jacket. He went over to look at Megan, head dropped onto her chest, limp and motionless in the arms of her dad.

He said to Alan, 'Hi, is that your daughter? Is she alright?'

We brought him up to date on the situation. Pat brought him coffee and biscuits. He wolfed down the biscuits.

I asked him how he had got on.

'It was good. No problems. I told you that I confirmed that Megan had dropped out of her studies on the phone. I went to the house where Glen had been living and interviewed the three girls he shared with. They were all students on the Performance Arts course. Gorgeous girls, dancers, willowy figures; Glen was a lucky lad living there. He kept it a bit quiet.'

'The girls did not want Glen to bring his friends to the place, they would have preferred the house to be all girls, but Glen actually owned the house. His parents had bought it for him for the duration of his stay. Afterwards to be sold. He charged them rent, I suppose, to pay off the mortgage, etc. Lots of parents do that sort of thing and often make a good profit at the end of the day.'

'There was no problem with Glen's finances. He was not a gambler or anything, so that was a dead end as a possible motive for his murder. I'm sorry, Alan, but it really looks like Megan and her gang were the guilty ones.'

This comment, of course, was a bombshell, but Alan did not really react, I don't think it sank in. He just carried on stroking the girl's hair.

'So, what's next?' Grant asked.

Chapter Thirty-Two

I said, in response to Grant's question, 'I think, my lads, we go to that squat and sort out those bastards. While we're there, we will pick up Megan's handbag and her mobile if it's there. What about it, guys?'

Ian and Grant grinned widely. 'Now you're talking, Ben!'

Pat said, 'I think you should wait until Megan wakes up, she may be difficult to control.'

'Fair enough,' I said. 'Well, while we wait, we can plan our campaign, then. Pens and paper needed.'

We didn't get a chance. Megan started to moan and cough. She gave a convulsive shake and rolled out of Alan's grip onto the floor on her back. She opened her eyes.

'Daddy!' She cried. 'My daddy!' She held out her arms pleadingly, tears streaming down her ravaged face. All of a sudden, she looked like a small child.

Alan picked her up. They locked together on the sofa in a fierce embrace. They were oblivious to me, or anyone else in the room. It was quite moving. Pat was also in tears. Even my eyes were a bit wet, I confess; it was the last thing I expected, this tender scene. Now what?

It was obvious we had to delay our raid on the squat; we could not leave Pat to cope with Alan and Megan by herself, of course.

We decided, as a group, to leave the room to Alan and his daughter on their own. So we trooped off to the other lounge on the other said of the house and left them alone.

I think we were all changing our minds about Megan. We all imagined some evil monster, a harlot, all teeth and claws tearing at us when she woke up. Instead, we had this vulnerable, pathetic little girl, clinging to her daddy. Was that Asian lad wrong? Surely this was no evil murderer who would have ordered Glen to be tortured and killed.

We sat there discussing the situation for a while, and then just tried to relax. I know we all found all this waiting very frustrating.

Then there came a tap on the door, which opened, and Alan strode in. He looked a different man altogether.

He whispered, 'Megan has gone back to sleep, but it is a normal sleep and she has a smile on her face. Could I ask another favour? Can you find a bedroom for her? I will undress her. Pat said she will help me. We might sponge her down and clean her up a bit.'

'Pat has bought a nightdress for her to wear. If we can put her in bed to sleep, it all off. I will sit with her, that's no problem, I don't want to sleep. I'm just so happy to have my little girl back. I can't tell you how grateful I am to you good folk.'

Pat followed Alan in. She said, 'Look, I'm fine, lads. You go off and sort out that squat. I know that's what you are aching to do.'

Ian said, hopefully, 'Are you sure?'

'Just go!'

So we did.

Chapter Thirty-Three

The situation at the squat was not like anything Ian and I had trained for, of course. This was a bunch of kids, unarmed, and off their heads with drugs, not a group of armed terrorists. *They really should be no trouble at all*, we thought, *apart from the problem of access inside*. We had been told, by the Asian lad, that the door was steel-backed and bolted and barred, even the police had failed to gain access.

In the car, Ian, sitting beside me in the front seats, asked, 'Have we a clear objective for this raid?'

I replied, 'The only clear objective we have is to get them to confess to the torture and killing of Glen Howard.'

'How to you imagine you will achieve that objective, Ben?'

I laughed. 'Haven't a clue, Ian. Play it by ear, I suppose.'

Ian said, 'They will all alibi each other, I bet. We won't be able to prove they were with Glen at the time of the murder, if that is known.'

'How the hell do the police ever manage to get a conviction at all, with the defence lawyers putting all sorts of obstacles in the way?'

'As said, we will have to play it by ear, mate. Something will turn up.'

'Hope springs eternal in the human breast. Anyway, I thought you wanted to blow them all up with dynamite, like that Asian kid suggested!'

'Yeah, well. It may come to something like that.'

We both laughed.

Grant and Ken in the back joined in the laughter.

I said, 'So when we get to the squat, I'll go and knock on the door and see what happens, yes? I don't imagine we'll be as lucky as Alan was, but you never know.'

'True.'

We left it at that.

We arrived eventually. It was, as expected, an old Victorian red brick building that looked like it had been a church hall. There was no church nearby, just houses. For some reason, this building had survived, just about. It looked very shabby and forlorn, windows boarded up, graffiti scrawled all over it.

We four large men strode up to the door at one end, and I, as I said I would, rapped my knuckles on the door. As expected, there was no response. I shoved against the door. It was absolutely solid, no doubt. I kicked it but it was a waste of time and energy. It would need a tank to break this door down. Hopeless trying.

Ian remembered what Grant had offered, telling us he worked as a roofer for his dad in the long holidays.

We looked expectantly at him. He grinned, then, like monkey he grabbed a drainpipe and started to climb. It took him no time at all to reach the roof and he swung on to it and disappeared. There followed lots of bangs and crashes, which we later learned was Grant using his steel-capped boots to good effect. His grinning big-chinned Desperate Dan face appeared looking down at us.

'Come on then,' he yelled.

So, we did. It was very easy. Victorian buildings have lots of ledges and such and the old cast iron drainpipe had sturdy fittings offering purchase to hands and feet.

We arrived at the top. Ken was puffing a bit, but he was older than us and a smoker, so no surprise there. But being an ex-marine, he was nevertheless well up to the task. Grant had kicked a hole in the roof, breaking a few slates.

One by one, we dropped through the hole into an attic of some kind. It was pitch dark, but Ken had a torch. He had brought it out of his car. I silently blessed him.

I was in my element. Action at long last! An adventure! Great.

I was a leader, so I gathered the three others together for a conflab.

I whispered, 'We must find a trap door, then I'll drop through first, and then Ian, Grant and Ken last. OK?'

Three heads nodded. I took Ken's torch.

We found the trap door easily enough, it was a big square solid piece of wood, covered with dust of ages. I opened it and some light came in from the room below, but we appeared to be above a sort of stage, curtained off from the rest of the room. The curtain was torn and gaping in places, letting through some flickering light, probably from oil lamps and candles. Almost certainly the electric supply had been cut off years ago.

It looked like a drop of ten to twelve feet below us. The stage, if that was what it was, was full of rubbish, boxes and bags of it, covered in dust. Some of the boxes were right underneath us, so would help cushion our fall, which was handy. So I jumped down without further ado, ready for battle.

I had an old service revolver down my jeans at the back, just to frighten them, it wasn't loaded as I had no ammo. Ian had a jack handle out of the Range Rover's tool bag, Grant had his steel-capped riding boots, and Ken his fists. I did not expect much opposition, to be fair. To be honest, I rather wished they would put up a fight!

The others dropped down. We were four big, angry men and we burst through the curtain and into the room. The gang were all there, right enough. They looked dumbfounded and in no state to fight us, much to all our disappointment. Just a bunch of stupid homeless layabouts. I suppose they couldn't help being the way they were.

Who knows what life had dished out to them? But they tortured and killed poor Glen. Because Megan had told them to, because she thought he was spying on her. Crazy and so sad. A bad decision on my part and another one on Glen's part, had led to a lovely lad's death...

All these thoughts ran through my head as I stood there confronting this pathetic gang. I thought fast.

I said, 'We have Souxie. She has confessed so there's no point in you telling us a bunch of lies.' I used my full Royal Navy Commander's voice. They literally quaked before me. I know I can be an impressive sight and sound. My ratings used to quake sometimes too, if I was angry.

One of the gang looked a little more intelligent than the rest.

I stood towering over him and almost touching him.

I thundered, 'You and your gang have tortured and murdered a young lad named Glen Howard. You will have to pay for your crime.'

This ragged goth creature whined, 'OK, OK, we didn't intend to kill him. Souxie told us to give him a kicking, but it turned bad, like, we were drunk, see, he snuffed it, so we had to stick him in the canal and stuff. He was a weakling, right? It wasn't our fault. Souxie made us do it. She scares the shit out of us. She is fucking evil, that bitch. I'm glad you've taken her the fuck away.'

The others nodded their heads in agreement.

Completely baffling. That pathetic little girl, crying in her daddy's arms?

An evil bitch. Really?

Ken had found a coil of rope on the stage. We tied all the gang together, sat on the floor, back-to-back. We sailors know a bit about ropes, they'd never untie themselves.

I went outside and rang the police. I told them the situation and they said they'd send round a squad as soon as they could to take over. I told them how I had got them to confess to the murder, and to follow that up and get statements from them as soon as they could. They must keep the pressure on, I said. I think they were furious, but they had no choice.

An hour passed. It seemed like eternity, but eventually, we heard sirens and saw flashing lights approaching. We piled into our car and left the scene, reasonably satisfied with our raid. Personally, I'd rather have tortured and killed the useless swine, but, hey! It's England. It's the twenty-first century, worse luck.

I thought it was all over. No way. Not by a long chalk.

Chapter Thirty-Four

We went back to my house, where Pat was waiting. We had got some cans of beer on the way to celebrate. Pat made some more coffee. We told her our tale and she was really relieved and happy for us. She told us Alan was sitting by Megan's side and she was asleep in a bedroom upstairs. The Crostons, my two staff, had returned and had gone to bed in their quarters. All was peaceful and quiet. Boring really.

We started on the beer, and I opened a bottle of good wine and we tried to be jolly and suchlike, to relieve the tension of the raid, I suppose, but it wasn't easy, as apart from Grant, we are not chatty people. After all, Glen had died. It was in the back of our minds, the elephant in the room. Nothing can ease that pain. Ever.

I yawned and looked at my watch. One twenty-four am. I started to get up, and was going to say something like, 'I'm off to bed, folks, stay here if you like.'

Suddenly, there was a terrifying scream and then another and yet another from upstairs. I bounded up the stairs, closely followed by the others. I burst into the bedroom where Alan was sitting with his daughter.

The sight that met my eyes was horrific. Blood splattered everywhere. Alan was lying bleeding on the carpet. Megan was standing over him, screaming her head off, with a pair of scissors in her hand. She rushed at me, her face an awful rictus of hate and fury.

I don't believe in evil spirits or possession, that sort of thing, although in the bible, Jesus did seem to spend a lot of his ministry casting out evil spirits and in parts of Africa possession is still routinely believed. However, to all appearances, what I was witnessing was a girl possessed by an evil spirit.

How else could a girl change from being a frightened little child reaching out for the protection of her beloved daddy to this vile creature that was now rushing towards me with murderous intent?

I didn't hesitate. I sidestepped to the left and punched Megan, directly on her mouth and chin. She collapsed at once, blood spurting from her cut lips. I knew she would be unconscious for some time, even though I had pulled my punch to some extent. She was just a young girl after all.

Ian, Pat and Grant rushed in behind me, understandably shocked and appalled by the scene. Pat ran over to Alan, who was groaning in pain. She yelled to Ian to call an ambulance. Grant started ripping up one of the sheets into strips.

I picked Megan up and dumped her unceremoniously on the bed. To my surprise, she woke up. She looked at me. And this was the most horrible thing that happened in my book. She spread her legs and through her split and bleeding lips, she smiled invitingly at me! I could have screamed in disgust and shock.

I took one of the strips of sheet and tied her legs together, then, with another strip, her arms. I was taking no more chances with this lunatic. She was writhing and screaming at me now, so I gagged her mouth as well.

Alan looked in a bad way. He had fainted and his breathing was shallow. Pat and Grant were doing their best to stop the bleeding, without much success.

Mr and Mrs Croston appeared. She rushed off to find a first aid box, but to my relief, the ambulance arrived in double-quick time. They took over from Pat and Grant and were their usual calm and professional selves. A really great service. They more than likely saved Alan's life that night.

Ian had also rung the police. Eventually, they arrived. They were pretty cool about the whole thing, actually. Calm and efficient. It took a lot of time and questions and statements then they carted Megan off to the station. A doctor had examined her and attended to her bleeding mouth. She had become sullen and had refused to speak. I never saw her again.

What a bloody awful night that had turned out to be. But it really was the beginning of the end.

Many months passed. The gang had been jailed for a very long time for murder. Megan had been found unfit to plead. She was certified insane and interred in a secure asylum for an unspecified period of time.

Alan had recovered from his injuries. We received a very generous cheque and a letter of thanks. He was obviously made of strong stuff, that man. How does any loving father cope with having such a daughter? Beats me.

Good news! Ian and Pat are now married and expecting a baby.

They are still running the agency and doing very well. I also help out when I can, but I am now quite enjoying being an Earl and in charge of the estate, the companies, the money.

I'm now thinking of going into pig rearing and showing. I've always liked pigs. I think most people do.

Romance? Still seeing Sue, spending weekends together alternating between Ireland and over here. She is building that house for us and still dropping lots of hints about marriage. I'm still thinking about that. I do love her. But I can't see why we need to marry. I don't think that it has anything about Sue becoming a countess if we do, but I'm really not sure…

THE END